To *MANFRED,*

Acknowledgmen

My grateful thanks to a long time friend Elizabeth for her help
and useful advice whilst editing this book, and her faith
in me finishing it. And to Rina for her help with ideas
for the plot, and for her patience during my writing it.

Chapter One.

Troubled Times

Ivan Garodny looked down at his swollen and bleeding feet as he hobbled along the rough path from his home, and wondered how he was going to perform at the city fete the following week. His spectacular dancing was one of the only ways he had of making ends meet, and now with the imminent birth of another child it would be a disaster if he couldn't perform. He knew that his wife Petra wouldn't be able to work much longer at her teaching job at the village school, and with things getting worse on the land the income from his few fields hardly seemed worth the effort that he put into them.

On August 4th 1904 their son Mikael was born into a land of poverty and uncertainty in a country that was about to tear itself apart not just then, but for many decades to come. The years of misrule and corruption that had gone on through the centuries were about to become even worse. The peasants of Russia were going to change forever the order of things in a way that would horrify the elite and ruling classes of that country. Ivan and his fellow workers were almost on the brink of starvation, ready for revolt in order to make changes to a system that rewarded the already rich landowners and supporters of Tsar Nicholas. Ivan counted himself as a happy and contented man until the latest farming problems started, and he could see thing were growing worse each passing day.

Just six months after the birth of his son there was a meeting called at the barn of a neighbour on the outskirts of Nizhnii Novgorod in order to set up a new workers council. This event was for obvious reasons kept very quiet as such political activities were quite illegal at that time. Ivan was one of the few peasant farmers to be trusted with the knowledge of the event, and was expecting to be voted on to the very secret committee that was about be formed. But as with most secrets it was leaked to just one ear too many and with disastrous results, the task of sorting the peasant problem out was given to Petr Arkadevich Stolypin Governor of the Province. His success with the peasants was to lead to his becoming Prime Minister the following year. It was due mainly to the fact that he had the police record of every male that lived in his province but to the peasants on his estates he seemed a reasonable enough man.

Ivan was for some reason being singled out as one of the leaders of the peasants most likely to be able to calm the situation, and Stolypin had been for many years following closely his career not just as a first rate dancer but the way he managed his smallholding. As one of the few reasonable landowners in the area Stolypin knew that with a little bit of persuasion Ivan just might bring some of the others to a more reasonable way of thinking. In other parts of Russia things weren't going quite so well there were stories of whole estates being burned and plundered every day.

How much the meeting between these two very different men would help to change the lives of those around them is difficult to ascertain but it most certainly helped to further Stolypin's career over the next few years. And so it was with nervous uncertainty that Ivan lifted the knocker on Stolypin's enormous front door. He glanced around hoping that none of the owner's estate workers had seen him arrive. It might cause him trouble with the workers committee to be seen sucking up to the estate owner.

There was nobody in sight, at least none that he could see but, who knows there could be workers in the huge barns watching his every move. After a few minutes the door opened and a serious looking Stolypin beckoned him inside, Ivan nervously followed him into the luxurious interior hall and opened the door to a study filled with huge bookcases and ornaments. He pointed to a chair near the desk for Ivan to sit on then sat opposite himself before speaking.

'Thank you for coming, Ivan. I hope that we can help each other with a few problems, I think you know just what I am talking about?' Ivan nodded 'Yes I do. And they are getting worse every day.'

Stolypin's face wore a worried look as he faced Ivan. 'How long have you worked on this estate Ivan?'

'About ten years roughly.'

'And have you been treated fairly well?'

'Yes I think so, that is better than most tenant farmers from around here.'

For the first time Stolypin smiled. 'That's good to hear, now let's get down to business. Now you know more than most people around here what's happening all over the country, and probably long before I do in some cases.'

Ivan nodded. 'Sometimes maybe.'

Stolypin shifted uneasily in his chair weighing up how he was going to gain this man's confidence. It wasn't going to be easy, he was, after all, a candidate for the local workers committee.

'Well as you and I know there are a lot of troublemakers around who'd like to see this country run differently, but who don't care how they achieve their aims. They have already ruined a lot of farms, burning the crops, looting, and killing their own kind.'

'Yes that's true.' replied Ivan. 'But a lot of farmers have been treated very badly in the past, and many of them are close to starvation. I know it's no excuse for a lot of what's been going on, but there are lunatics among them who will stop at nothing.'

Stolypin nodded in agreement. 'Well, Ivan, this country can be a great place to live in if only citizens would talk reasonably together, like you and I are doing today. Don't you agree?'

Ivan didn't like the way this conversation was going but he managed to nod agreement all the same. 'What exactly do you want me to do then?' Stolypin paused a moment. 'Well without putting yourself too much at risk just let me know when to expect trouble, that's all.'

'And what do I get out of it if I agree?'

'I will cut your rent by half, and give you my word that I'll guarantee you a good return on your crop. How does that sound to you?'

Ivan smiled and held out his hand. 'It's a deal but a very risky one on my part. If anything goes wrong my head will be on the block together with my family, as well you must know.' Ivan noticed at this point that Stolypin's right hand was covered in bandages so he withdrew his in case this caused embarrassment.

'What's happened to your hand ?'

'Just a small problem. My brother was killed a few weeks ago in a gun duel so as a result I also fought the same man and came off worse, it was a matter of honour.'

Ivan shook his head in dismay. 'That's bad. You must rest it now.' Stolypin nodded then moved his left hand towards Ivan and shook his warmly 'Good! That's done then. If anyone asks why you've come here today tell them I've asked you to dance at my daughter's party next month.'

'Is that what you want?'

'Yes of course! Aren't you the best dancer in these parts?'

'I'm glad you think so.'

'I do, and I've already booked the musicians. They've worked with you many times already. One thing puzzles me, Ivan. Having watched you dance on many occasions, where did you learn to dance like that?' Ivan paused a moment and smiled. 'Many years ago an uncle of mine paid for me to study at the Imperial School of Ballet at the Mariinsky Theatre for two years, but he ran short of money so I never finished the course. Anna Pavlova was there at the time but she was fortunately state funded and is the prima ballerina now.'

Stolypin looked surprised at this revelation and resolved to really help this obviously talented man in his employ to enjoy a better standard of living.'That's very sad. You were obviously meant to be more than a common farmer and that's a fact.'

Ivan by now was looking slightly more relaxed and the worried look had left his face, this was the first time that he'd felt his employer was really going to help him in more ways than one. He was reasonably certain that providing he played his cards right at least he'd be better off than most of the local farmers, the risk he'd be running was another thing. Perhaps he'd better ask just one small favour.

'Just supposing I get serious problems at some point, what then?'

Stolypin thought a moment. 'I will take steps to see that you and your family are removed from the area to a safe place at my expense, no matter what it costs me.'

'Thank you. That was the only thing that was troubling me, some of my friends would think me a traitor if they suspected anything.'

Stolypin rose from the desk smiling. 'That's settled then. I look forward to hearing something from you when and if problems get worse. Many thanks for coming and give my regards to your family won't you?'

Ivan rising from his chair nodded, and followed Stolypin out of the room then left the house his mind buzzing with thoughts of what the immediate future held for him. The deed was done. From now on there was no turning back.

By the time he'd got back to his own farm some miles away his feet were really troubling him and he wondered just how he would be able to perform at the next village function, which was only two weeks away. This was one of the most important events in the country and certainly the most lucrative engagement he'd ever been booked for. The fair was to be part of the First Congress of the Moslem Union to press for social and economic reforms for Moslem people in Russia. He looked down at his feet as he neared his home and the state of his worn shoes said it all, no wonder he was having trouble walking even the string holding them together was coming apart. The rough pathway leading to his home was certainly giving him a lot of pain in his legs and feet, especially now that the ground was so hard owing to the lack of rain.

He paused and sat down on a grassy patch for a rest and to catch his breath. The warm sun on his back made him a little drowsy. His mind went back to the days of his youth when he'd been training for the ballet, he really thought that somehow his hard work would pay off in the end. He certainly worked much harder than most of the other pupils and never stopped looking for perfection, and his unique dancing was admired by all of the company. He shook his head and looked down at the legs and feet that were now old and sore, and longed for the days past when he never stopped dancing.

Chapter Two

The Meeting

The barn was filled with peasant farmers from all the surrounding area and on the door were very aggressive looking labourer's. Who were there to stop anyone entering not known to them. There was a buzz of excitement in the place as the meeting began, the election of the first committee was only a formality, as all the persons involved had been already decided upon. This was certainly going to be a day to remember by all those present and the mix of personalities was very varied. Ivan knew that he would be one of the few moderates present and it was going to be difficult to get his views accepted by most of them. They were certainly going to be a tough bunch to deal with and would not be put off taking drastic action against crop raiders and greedy landowners.

There were already very helpful guidelines that had been laid down by other groups in the country following on from the January "Bloody Sunday" demonstration in St Petersburg. The main case for calling this meeting was for lower farm rents to offset the demands for higher labour wages. Ivan took a seat at the back of the barn but close enough to be able to hear most of what was about to be discussed. He was slightly deaf in one ear but never complained or let others know about it.

The first thing they had to decide was the election of a leader and after a lot of discussion they decided on Sergei Anikin, a burly farm tenant who was always a help to any farmer in dispute with his landowner. The meeting went quite smoothly and it was decided that an ultimatum should be given to all landowners to either to lower the rents or all payments to them would be stopped. They had heard about the worker's strikes in most of the towns and cities so felt that the time was ripe for action. Even the army and navy were on the brink of mutiny after the unsuccessful war against Japan, but this had been quietly crushed and the majority of the armed forces remained loyal to the government. The casualties of the war were evident in every town and city in the land. The recent general train strike that had been so well organized sadly came to nothing, and a lot of the participants had been rounded up and imprisoned.

Ivan sat there listening to all the arguments for and against this peasant revolt wondering what if anything he would report back to Stolypin. He guessed that he would probably get to know most of it anyway from other sources. The man sitting next to Sergei looked very out of place indeed, it was obvious he wasn't from the local district, his clothes and shoes were that of a town dweller. He looked more like a prosperous western businessman. He was definitely not one of them at all and was listening intently to every word that was spoken, before eventually being introduced by Sergei as Leon Trotski a guest speaker for the worker's movement.

This small bearded man stood up, glanced at his notes, then looked around the table and started to speak.

'Good morning comrades. I have been asked to speak to you all today just to let you know that we in the cities are with you in the struggle for a better life. You have probably wondered why this meeting today has been kept so secret. I have unfortunately just spent two years in prison in Siberia for my political beliefs. However that is now in the past and the future looks slightly better for us all. The day is close when the ordinary people of this country of ours will be masters of our own destiny and the parasites who have lived so well off us will have to pay the price of their past injustices to us. All over our land different sections of the community are at this very moment getting ready to right the wrongs of the past, and very soon the reckoning is coming. All those supporting the Tsar and his followers will be removed and we my friends will all be equal in this land of ours. There will be lots of blood shed before we win our freedom but it will be worth it in the end. We the workers of this land of ours will triumph of that there is no doubt, and we owe it to our descendants to make sure it happens. We are only at the start now but I can assure you we will win this struggle against the imperialists and their ill-gotten wealth. I wish this meeting and you all good luck and thank you for allowing me to speak briefly to you today.'

As he sat down there was a murmur of approval from the peasant farmers and a smiling Sergei stood up to congratulate Trotski on his speech. 'Thank you, comrade, for taking the trouble to be with us today and there is no doubt that we will try and follow your great example in the struggle that is about to come.' When the meeting finally came to an end Ivan began to realize fully who the man was who had joined them that day, he had through the years heard at different times news of this man Trotski's clashes with the establishment and his final imprisonment. The outcome of the voting for the committee left Ivan out, but he was allowed to sit in at future meetings as an adviser, being one of the oldest and most trusted tenant farmers. So at least he'd have first hand knowledge of future moves in the workers struggle for independence.

Although Ivan left the meeting feeling slightly more hopeful about his future there was a nagging mistrust of what he'd just heard he'd give it a few more months then decide what to do. Petra was always telling him not to poke his nose into the things that always brought trouble in the end. And Petra was nearly always right she thought things through not like him at all. Perhaps it was a good thing that he hadn't been voted onto the main committee after all, he was relieved that now no blame could be attached to him for the outcome of any troubles. He was now fortunately in a better position to report to Stolypin without the staunch members of the workers committee watching his every move.

Chapter Three

The Fair

On Ivan's return home Petra was standing waiting at the door eager to question him about the outcome of the meeting. But he was in no mood to reveal too much to her, he just knew that she might let slip something to a friend. She eyed him suspiciously, arms folded. 'That must have been a good meeting? You've been gone for hours.' She said.

Ivan shrugged his face was very grim. 'Nothing much happened, just a lot of talk that's all. The usual old rubbish with a lot of them moaning about life in general.'

'And I suppose you're on the committee once again then?'

'Not this time. They never even mentioned my name, but they'll want my advice from time to time no doubt.'

Petra looked at him in amazement, she'd never known him not to be directly involved in the farmers problems before, this was indeed a relief to her. Perhaps he was getting too old for these matters maybe the younger ones had different ideas to his, better to let them get on with it she thought.

As they went into the house Petra decided to change the subject and try and cheer him up a little.

'How are your feet today Ivan? I've got some special ointment for you, it's supposed to be very good, but it takes at least a week to have any effect.'

Ivan sat down on a chair and took off one of his badly worn boots, not only did they have holes in them but the woolen socks as well. His foot was now swollen and sore, so bad that he was reduced to walking at about half his normal pace.

He pulled off his sock and examined the foot more closely at the same time shaking his head. Petra moved closer and lifted it up to examine it.

'This is terrible, Ivan, let me get some water, and when you've washed them I'll try the ointment on them, take your other boot off and just sit there a moment.'

In the sparsely furnished kitchen Petra took the ointment from a drawer and filled a bowl from the pitcher of water, she then returned to the living room and placed the bowl next to Ivan's feet. He slowly placed them in the water to soak too frightened to touch them as they were both covered in blood.

'How am I going to carry on like this Petra? I must get some new boots soon. This is a crazy life we're living here there must be a better way.'

She sighed and bent down to bathe his feet gently trying hard to hold back the tears from her eyes.

'Next week I will make sure you get some new boots before you go to dance at the city fair, my love.'

Ivan winced as she moved her hands around his sore feet wondering just how he was going to be fit enough to walk properly never mind dance at the fair.

The following week having had a fair amount of rest thanks to Petra doing more than her share of the work on the farm, Ivan was feeling fitter and in a much more positive mood. As they loaded the cart with all the children and enough food for the journey he eyed his new leather boots with satisfaction. They were the best and most expensive ones he'd ever possessed, they were now highly polished and gleaming and he couldn't wait to dance in them. He had of course worn them a few times to take the stiffness out and make sure they didn't hurt his feet. This he felt was going to be one of the best and memorable days of his life, there were reports of record crowds gathering for the grand carnival. The journey was quite a long one involving the crossing of two bridges and very narrow roads.

They were surrounded by thousands of other families on the same road all going to the fair, hoping that this event would be the most exiting event of the year. The City of Nizhnii Novgorod was the fourth largest area after Moscow with a huge population for a northern city. Ivan and Petra had only visited it once before, never having had the money for extravagances on that scale.

The children were of course buzzing with excitement at the prospect of meeting other children and perhaps a ride on the fairground machines. They were all dressed in what was at that time their Sunday best, clothes that had been bought in the village market for special occasions. The youngest Mikael watched as the other children chattered endlessly about what they thought would happen at the fair. The oldest Anna, said that she'd heard from her friends at school that there would be fire-eaters, jugglers, clowns, and elephants performing. And to top it all father was being paid to dance at a special Muslim festival, a rare feat for someone not one of them. Even the great ballet dancer Pavlova had never performed at such an event as this. The chatting went on and on until they came to the bridge over the river where all eyes were on the swirling current passing underneath.

The river was in full stream owing to the recent heavy rains, the banks were bursting and the level of the water almost touching the underside of the bridge. Ivan realizing that the horse would probably not be able to haul all of them over the hump of the bridge stopped at the foot of it. He'd watched others struggling to cross it and decided to unload the children and Petra to make the cart lighter. This seemed to do the trick. They then got across it quite comfortably, and went on to finish the journey before dusk.

On arriving at the festival site the whole area was buzzing with families preparing their makeshift tents for their stay, it was certainly going to be a merry sleepless night. These people knew how to enjoy themselves on such an occasion, good times were in short supply in the community then. Ivan soon sorted out a sheltered spot next to some trees and they made themselves comfortable.

The next day was spent exploring the town and the children gazed in wonderment at not only the fabulous buildings, but also the sight of so many different acts and attractions of the artistic performers scattered around everywhere.

Ivan later took them to the headquarters of the organizing committee for the Moslem congress to confirm his arrival and it was a man named Abdur Rashid Ibrahim who greeted him warmly. They confirmed his fee and promised payment on completion of his act the following night. They also gave him a copy of the programme of events at the festival, and tickets for the rest of his family to be present on the night he danced for them. The way the programme was listed confirmed his suspicion that he was one of the highest paid artists of the night, this certainly made him feel good indeed.

Although as a Christian he didn't agree with some of the objects of the Moslem leadership it was good that they were going in the same direction as his people. Perhaps now things were going to get better for him and his family.

On the way back they passed a large group of people watching a man rehearsing his bear dancing act, the children standing open mouthed, obviously never having seen such a sight before. It was maybe just a taste of what was to come over the next few days, the children would certainly have something to talk about when they got back home.

The next day seemed a never-ending one for Ivan although the children found plenty to watch, and there was lots going on around the fairground to amuse them. He put his new shoes on several times to make sure that they wouldn't hurt him during his dance routine, they certainly felt better than the first time he put them on. As the day wore on even the children seemed to tire a little so the whole family settled down for an afternoon nap. Ivan knew that the evening's dance routine would need all his energy and concentration, this would have to be the best performance of his life. His reputation as a dancer was really at stake, he couldn't leave anything to chance as other bookings might result from this event.

Later that evening as the family made their way towards the concert area. They were amazed at the crowds that were going their way, surely the place didn't hold this many? At the entrance the stewards checked their tickets and one of them showed Ivan to the artist's changing rooms. He then showed them their stage-side seats for the performance, they were certainly good ones. With over two hours to go before his part Ivan

m to watch the rest of the entertainment and it was really
The dancing was certainly different from anything he'd ever
ot of the songs were in a language he'd not come across

About fifteen minutes before he was about to go on stage Ivan left the family to talk to the musicians backstage to let them know his requirements, they had worked with him many times in the past and knew exactly what he wanted of them. He then went back to the dressing room to put on his shoes and stage outfit, it was then that he noticed that his hands were shaking slightly. He had never had this happen to him before, it was the first time that he'd been this nervous. He put it down to the fact that this was definitely the largest crowd he'd ever danced for. As he entered the stage area the crowd clapped loudly. They seemed to know that they were in for an extraordinary performance, some of them must have watched him before.

There was a moment's silence before the band started to play and Ivan began to dance with the full glare of the stage lights on him. The audience sat riveted in their seats, some of them had never seen such dancing before in their lives, and probably wouldn't ever again. After about fifteen minutes Ivan began to perspire and the sweat began to trickle down his face slow at first then more as the time went on. The night was a warm one and he felt slightly more overdressed than usual, but at least he looked smart which was more than some of the other acts did.

As he finished his routine the audience stood up and clapped endlessly. He bowed and had to return twice to the stage before they stopped applauding. His dancing had obviously really pleased them no end.

Back at the dressing room the organizer congratulated him, paid him his fee and said he'd be in touch the following year when they had the next convention. Ivan thanked him profusely then changed and went back to his family to watch the last act.

On the way back home he quietly told Petra that he'd been paid. This made her a very happy woman, now they could pay off a lot of their debts and eat reasonably well for the next few weeks. Life was beginning to look a little better for the family now perhaps their luck was about to change.

Chapter Four

More Trouble

It was late one night a few weeks later that Ivan woke up on hearing strange noises coming from somewhere close, there was also a smell of smoke coming from under the door. He quickly dressed and ran outside just in time to see a ball of fire in the distance. As he rounded the barn it was evident that there were several fields on fire including some of his own, putting the fire out was out of the question as it was already spreading further and had reached his neighbour's farm. Fortunately the wind was coming from behind his house and the barn so at least they were reasonably safe at present.

He walked slowly towards his fields and looked sadly at the damaged crops hardly able to believe what had happened, this was no accident someone had maliciously set fire to the field. He moved on determined to find out what his neighbour was doing maybe he could be of some help, his own crop was ruined with nothing left but stubble. Ivan first went back to the house to make sure that Petra hadn't been awakened by the crackle of the fire and wondered where he was, but she and the children were still fast asleep just as he'd left them. That was at least a blessing. This was just like a bad dream one that if it wasn't for the smell he somehow might wake up from any minute. It was the end of his dreams of making a life for himself and his family in Russia. Surely things couldn't get any worse. As he left the house and passed the barn one glance inside convinced him that at least he had enough hay stored to feed the cattle for a few weeks. He then moved quickly on towards his neighbours farm to see if help was needed there, the flames had passed all his land by this time and everything was black and a smouldering mess.

The scene at the next farm was chaos with everyone passing buckets of water in a chain from the nearby river, so without a word Ivan joined them in their frantic efforts to quench the roaring flames. It took well over an hour to keep the fire from reaching the barns holding some of the livestock and feed, this was an achievement as the fire was engulfing all the rest of the nearby crops. Having saved the barns they then concentrated on the section surrounding the house itself as the flames moved ever closer. It took over two hours to quell the flames creeping ever closer to the house and the heat was beginning to have it's effect on them, they were getting slower moving the water onto the fire.

As the dawn broke the fire had moved on relentlessly consuming field after field in its path, leaving behind burnt and smoking stubble in it's wake. Ivan together with his neighbour's gathered in the farmhouse exhausted from their efforts, it was still dark outside but another day was dawning. He decided to make his way back home. Maybe Petra was still sleeping and wasn't aware of what had been happening, he certainly hoped so.

Chapter Five

The Reckoning

Within days of the fire happening Ivan had made up his mind that things couldn't possibly get any worse, all his crops were burnt and there was very little left in the barns. There was certainly not enough food left to get them or their animals through the coming cold winter.

His thoughts were just what should be done to avoid almost certain starvation for his family and nearby relations, he decided to first of all approach Petr Stolypin for advice bearing in mind what his offer had been some time before. He certainly couldn't see his entire family moving on somewhere else with only one horse and cart between them. He had carefully given his boss little snippets of information over the past few months, just enough to satisfy his political friends need to know what was going on in the immediate area.

A few days later Ivan called at Stolypin's house to request help to flee the country knowing that serious problems were about to overtake them. He had of course alerted his relatives of his intention to go and advised them to leave everything and join him.

Petr Stolypin knowing what the situation was with his tenants had been expecting this. The information that Ivan had passed him over the troubled period had been used to formulate a plan by the elite landowners of the area to combat the renegade peasants and crush the rebellion.

Both men although miles apart in status had a healthy respect for one another, Ivan felt that he could trust his boss within reason and that he'd so far never lied to him. Stolypin also felt that Ivan was a reasonably honest hard working person whom he felt obliged to help now that things were going seriously wrong. As they faced each other in the huge room that was richly furnished and crowded with expensive large paintings each was aware of the huge gap in their living circumstances.

Stolypin was the first to speak knowing exactly the reason for Ivan's call, he knew that he was about to lose one of his most trusted tenant farmers.

'I think I know why you've come to see me Ivan.'

Ivan nodded. "Yes I suppose so. Things have got much worse in the last few weeks and my family and I are definitely going to move on somewhere else.'

'Where are you heading for then?'

'France, that's if we can make it.'

Stolypin looked puzzled. 'That's quite a journey to make especially with young children.'

'Yes I know but we've thought it all out and if we avoid the highest mountains we'll make it somehow.'

Stolypin rose and walked towards a book shelf took down a larger than average book and returned to his desk.

'I can let you have copies of the latest maps of all the areas that you will pass through.. Also I'll give you a letter that may help with your safe passage through the first stages of your journey.'

'Thank you but there is something else that we need badly.'

' You mean transport?'

'Yes. We've only got one horse and cart, and there are eleven of us in my immediate family.'

'You've been a good tenant and very helpful over the years so I'll let you have another good horse and cart, and as much food as you can carry. How will that suit you?'

Ivan smiled for the first time that morning. 'That would be a great help for us, thank you. My family will really be grateful to you.'
Stolypin rose and shook Ivan's hand warmly. 'Let me know when you are ready and how much food you want and I'll have the horse delivered. I'll be sorry to see you go but wish you all luck in your journey.' He paused a moment thoughtfully reflecting what to say next.

'Many of the things that you've told me over the last few months have helped me no end to make reforms for the workers of this country of ours. One day you will realize how much things will have changed in Russia.' Ivan thanked him again and left feeling better than he had for some time. Perhaps now things were going his way and he was moving on to a better life. But it was going to be a long and perhaps dangerous journey.

The next few weeks were spent planning the forthcoming journey into unknown territory, it was a surprise to Ivan that not all the relatives were prepared to make the trip. Two of them said they were satisfied with life in Russia and thought that life was going to get better if the much-talked about revolution succeeded. Ivan thought they were fools and told them so in no uncertain terms. With two days to go before leaving Ivan collected the other horse and cart loaded with provisions and animal feed and a rifle and ammunition from the Stolypins stables. He had gazed in amazement at the amount the landowner had given him, it certainly should last them a few weeks almost enough to get them to Poland. Shaking hands Ivan thanked him most profusely this was indeed a great way of rewarding him for his many years of service. The horse certainly looked in better shape than his own one and even its shoes were brand new.

In Ivan's cart was wife Petra, two year old Mikael, Nika aged four, and Anna aged seven. The other larger cart held Yuri Ivan's younger brother, his wife Olga, son Dmitri aged three, Natalya aged five, Konstantin aged seven, and Galina eleven. The lack of education of the children on the journey wasn't thought to be a huge problem, as their schooling up to this point had been very rudimentary. And with Petra now their full time teacher she would see to it that they didn't miss out on anything during the journey. Yuri was a completely different sort of man to his brother, much bigger and altogether stronger through years of rough farmwork and with a very weather beaten face.

Although two years younger than Ivan he did look very much older in appearance. His ambitions were very limited having lived a life of poverty all the years before in Russia but despite it all with a strong family around him he had been reasonably happy. His wife Olga was his main strength and had worked hard since their marriage to keep the farm going especially when the harvests had been bad ones. She had been born into a reasonably wealthy family but they disowned her when she announced her intention to marry a relatively poor farmer. Their first born Galina was a very happy child and brought them great joy and as she grew up it was fantastic the way she helped look after the other three children. But with four children Yuri and Olga really did struggle at times so now this journey really meant a lot to them both, they had high hopes of a much better life in another country.

Chapter Six

The Journey

On that day in September 1906 when they all left Ivan looked at his almost empty house with sadness, there wasn't much left that was worth anything, and even the things that they were taking didn't add up to anything of value. For a lifetime's work he was still a poor man but at least he had reasonably good health and a loving family around him, and perhaps with God's help they would all survive the long trip to a new land and a better life. The only money he had to take was the fee he'd been paid a few weeks earlier for his dancing at Stolypin's house party, this was going to be a life saver if things got hard for them. It was also fortunate that all the adult members of the family were of farming background and could work if the need arose. Time was not important but winter was close and they needed to get past all the mountain ranges and into a warmer climate by the spring, otherwise the younger children might become ill.

By the end of the first day they had only covered about thirty miles and the children were looking a bit weary, so when a suitable piece of waste ground appeared they decided to camp there for the night. Being fully aware of the danger of wild animals when sleeping outdoors both the male members kept watch with a loaded gun ready for any emergency. They also gathered wood and lit a fire not only to cook on but also to keep hungry wolves and bears away, they then took it in turns to keep watch throughout that long and cold night.

Nothing unusual happened during the night and when the dawn broke they ate and made ready to move on, hoping to cover a bit more ground than the previous day. The children were still as exited at this great adventure and couldn't wait to see all the places that they'd only read about in books. About an hour into the journey they heard a loud growl and spotted a huge bear at the edge of the forest but it took one look at them and decided to move off elsewhere. This was a relief as killing a bear at this stage would not only have delayed them but they didn't need any extra food yet, the carts were fully loaded so much so that the risk involved didn't justify thinking about it. This second day went well and they covered a lot more distance than the previous one even though there was no rush to get anywhere special. Ivan like his relatives didn't need a compass because as experienced farmers they knew exactly where they were at all times, aided with the help of the detailed maps given them by Stolypin.

At the end of day three they had reached the border of Belorussia and the going then became a little more difficult, the roads were rougher and the forests much more dense. It was colder inside these forests as the sun couldn't penetrate and it was certainly very damp, this they overcame by putting on more clothing. Ivan found this most uncomfortable especially having to sit for hours on the cart which rocked and swayed over the rough roads.

The only incident that bothered them over the next few days was when a group of vicious looking men armed with knives suddenly appeared on the road in front demanding money. They soon took flight when faced with a rifle pointed at them, these men didn't wait to see if it was loaded. It was at this point in the journey that small animals such as rabbits and young deer were helping with their daily food supply. Such things had been an everyday part of their way of life in Russia, and they had brought their traps with them. The food supply was by now going down a little and from now on they needed to add to it, their assumption that it would last until reaching Poland looked a bit unlikely.

Each night after the children had fallen asleep the parents discussed the progress made and checked the next days route. They somehow felt that the condition of the roads and paths would not improve much until they reached the large towns well into Poland. Their knowledge and experience of wild plant life and what to eat of it would now be most important as this was not good farming land that they were passing through. They made sure that this skill was passed on to the older children for maybe future use.

Chapter Seven

Poland

After travelling for seven weeks the group finally reached the border of Poland and this land much to their surprise was not unlike their own, the people there seemed a lot happier although still just as poor. To eke out their meagre food supplies some of the family worked for the small farms in return for anything that was available. This obviously slowed them down somewhat but it kept them all from starvation. They only needed to do the few odd jobs the local farmers were pushed to find time for at the end of the harvest season, and the children were pleased to make friends with the local youngsters.

The weather was beginning to change now and the nights were getting much colder, even the children were starting to complain of the cold at times. One piece of luck they had was that a farmer suggested that Ivan showed his dancing talents to a local show organizer, this resulted in a one night booking for him. His fee kept them all in food for over a week. They found the country was very pleasant and the people most friendly so there was no hurry to pass through it, so they just ambled on and really enjoyed the experience. The only problem that they encountered was whilst going down a steep rough hill the axle snapped on Ivan's cart, this they managed to repair with a tree branch until a proper repair was carried out at the next village.

Petra was making sure that the children didn't miss out on their education and spent at least two hours every day giving them lessons. She also made sure that they knew the different plants and wild vegetables they regularly ate, this was going to play an important part in their future lives. At every reasonable opportunity they picked and tasted all the plants she pointed out to them along the way.

With a change in the weather and the first falls of snow appearing on the roads, they decided to try and find a kind farmer who would let them stay in a barn until it got a bit warmer. Their luck was in as at the very next farm there were quite a few empty barns and the farmer and his family were more than glad of the company. Especially when they found out the visitors were also great entertainers as well, music and dancing was an everyday happening with them. The next few weeks were happy ones and the time passed very quickly so when it came time to say farewell the children shed a few tears, they certainly enjoyed the rest at the farm.

Before leaving they had news of what was now going on in Russia. It seemed that the Tsar Nicholas had appointed Petr Stolypin as his Prime Minister of the Interior to try to quell the peasants uprising. He had brought in new measures to appease the tenant farmers and give them more rights to the land they farmed. These new measures seemed to be working at first but there were a few hotheads who were not satisfied and groups of them were hell bent on a full-scale revolution. Any doubts that Ivan and his family had about leaving were dispelled at this news, they had all felt certain things were going to get much worse. Ivan felt secretly that at least he'd done his bit to present the farmers side of the problem to Stolypin in the months before leaving. There were also unconfirmed rumours that Stolypin had brought about the imprisonment of thousands of troublemakers in the last few weeks. It was also whispered that over a thousand of them had already been hanged as revolutionaries. Ivan wondered what had changed his ex employer to take such drastic actions.

And so on they went a little more refreshed, full of hope and glad to have escaped it all, even though the roads were now getting a little hillier in places. Although the shortest route after they left Poland was through the main part of Germany to France they decided to go slightly south to avoid as many hills as possible. This meant a slight detour south but it was hopefully going to be worth it as the route they'd chosen was slightly a flatter one. Going anywhere near the alps was out of the question at this time of the year, as they usually closed them anyway. As they neared the border with Germany news was that the alpine roads were indeed closed to all traffic and big detours were being used.

Just before reaching the border itself they came across another group of Russians who were also fleeing to what they hoped was a better life. They were in a most distressed state because both their parents had passed away on the journey. They explained that as they were now so short of money they'd buried them both in the forest nearest where they'd died. They were also unfortunately down to their last bit of food, Ivan's group gave them a little for which they thanked them most profusely. They had some spare boots and clothing taken from the parent's bodies before burying them, these were offered in return for the food. Ivan thanked them for the kind offer but only took the fathers boots as a gesture of goodwill.

Chapter Eight

Germany

There were no problems at the border and the German guards there were more than helpful when they were informed that the whole party was bound for France. They told them that things were getting much worse day by day in Russia and they were wise to leave when they did. With so many children included they were astonished that they'd traveled all the way from Russia. Once across the border all roads seemed to lead to main towns but they wisely decided to avoid these as life in the rural areas would be much better, and camping out in the towns might prove very difficult if not impossible.

The major problem from then on was the language as none of them could either speak or write German, but they got by most of the time with signs and bits of what they heard along the way. This was where the children excelled most of all, as they seemed to pick up things much quicker than the parents did. So when real trickier situations arose they were more than pleased to make use of their newly found skills.

At night when they made camp all the children would huddle together and discuss all the new words that they had discovered that day, and even the youngest one Mikael was surprisingly picking it all up too. By the second week in Germany the children had got most of the main words right and this was to be most helpful to them in later life.

By trying to avoid the mountain ranges and keep to the more sheltered valleys the distance they were covering was obviously a lot greater than expected. Especially when avoiding cities like Berlin the detours were enormous at times. This delay was to prove most beneficial when as they got near the French border it was Christmas time and a farmer there invited them home for a very festive lunch and evening meal. They certainly all ate well and hoped that their small payment towards the food and a musical contribution to the festivities was well recieved. Ivan crowned the occasion by giving them a most dazzling display of his dancing, one that left the German family gasping. They thanked their hosts and family for the great time they had there and left for the few remaining miles to the French border, and somewhere suitable in France was to be the end of their long journey. Their hopes of settling there spurred them on they had heard from others that it was a good place to live in, certainly much better and more civilized than Russia was when they left it.

By this point Ivan and his younger brother Yuri were both feeling much better and rested despite the trip being a bit trying at times, it was almost a rest after all the years they'd slogged away on the farm. After their meal and the children tucked up in bed the parents all sat around the log fire, and started to discuss what they thought about the last stage of the journey into France the following day.

Ivan stared into the fire very thoughtfully before speaking.

'How far into France do you think we should go?'

The others looked at each other in silence. Yuri was the first to answer.

'Until we find a suitable place to stay. That's all.'

Petra nodded in agreement. 'Yes and I think that we should look for somewhere near a fairly large town just in case we need a job to keep us in food until we sort ourselves out.'

'Like Paris you mean?' Replied Olga.

'Not really! That's too big but a town with farms around it. A place we could help out in for a start.' Said Petra.

Ivan moved the logs back on the fire that had rolled off. 'I think that we'd better wait and see what the country is like before we make any decisions'. He said.

Galina, Yuri's oldest girl, was not yet asleep and was listening intently to all this talk, trying to conjure up what sort of life was in store for them all in the years to come. This was all very exiting and learning another language was going to be fun for them.

Chapter Nine

France

The aim of the journey towards the final destination was to be in a slow and methodical direction towards somewhere north east of Paris and this took quite a few days. They knew that finding some sort of employment was to be a crucial part of the plan, but what sort of work there was in that part of France they were unsure about. But they were lucky in that by asking around the villages they found out that further along the route was a large town that might suit them down to the ground. It was called Metz and not only were there plenty of farms in the area, it was also a manufacturing place with factories employing hundreds of workers. It was a town that over the years had became hotly disputed territory as it was the first major industrial area between Germany and France, and it had changed hands many times over the years.

And so they made their way towards the town it certainly sounded the right sort of place to live in, and as a bonus there was also a huge travellers area on the outskirts. They were not in a financial position to live in a house of any sort at that point in time, so they sought out the site and selected a large vacant spot under some trees. During their first few days there the whole family were delighted to have found what they thought was their final resting place. The journey was now over and they could settle down and relax in what seemed like a peaceful country.

During the first few weeks they managed to find the odd day,s work in local factories and railway yards, the pay wasn't much but they managed to get by on it. The children, with the exception of the youngest Mikael, were all enrolled at the nearby school, and although nervous at first not knowing the language very soon got the hang of it, unlike their parents who really struggled with it. It was now spring and with the weather getting warmer some of the family started exploring the nearby town and it's surroundings.

The place certainly was an exiting one in many ways and there was something to please each and everyone in the family including Ivan. It was he who discovered a huge theatre in the centre of town sensitively converted from an original army ammunition storage building. It was unlike any other theatre he'd ever seen before so he went inside to explore the place. He was lucky that on that day they were having the first rehearsal for the year, it was also his luck that nobody had stopped him from entering by the front door. Just inside the entrance hall he stood gazing at the impressive list of past performers that had appeared there since it had been converted to a theatre. At this point in time this had been less than twenty years.

Once inside he stood quietly looking at some of the dancers warming up for what looked like some sort of audition. As nobody seemed to be troubled by his presence there he then moved towards the front of the stage and sat down. The whole interior of the building was stunning with ceiling artwork and gilding everywhere, and the stage area itself ornately decorated to a very high standard.

The man seated closest to the stage in the center looked most interested in what they were doing and he was calling them on in turn. Ivan studied the dancers and their movements as each one performed their piece, to him they seemed very polished but he somehow felt that he even in his unfit state could certainly do much better. Finally when the last one had finished the man watching them glanced around and saw Ivan sitting there, he beckoned him over and said something in French that Ivan didn't quite understand. Having been unable to converse properly the man then called for an interpreter. They managed to find one who spoke a bit of Russian. It seemed that the company were short of dancers that season and were looking for new talent.

When the interpreter found out that Ivan had been a former pupil at the Mariinsky Ballet School he passed this on to the director whose facial expression immediately changed. This was indeed a bonus perhaps he'd now witness some real dancing if this stranger could be persuaded to audition for them. Although the man looked a little old for first class ballet dancing who knows what hidden talent he might uncover, and there seemed to be a shortage of it at the moment.

Ivan of course appeared delighted to show off his skills but asked for their patience whilst he warmed up a little backstage, this they agreed to readily hoping to see maybe something different. After all he was Russian and they were rated as some of the best dancers in the world.
After borrowing some tights and reasonably fitting shoes from the stores Ivan began his warm up routine backstage watched by a small group of dancers, they certainly looked on with curious interest at his movements. Although a little jerky at times he was certainly very artistic and so different from any they'd ever seen before. After about fifteen minutes he signaled that he was ready to perform and the director and most of the others watched as Ivan moved onto the center of the stage. He had selected a recording that was familiar to him.

At first there was nothing unusual about his routine and it looked just like a continuation of his warm up, then all of a sudden things changed, he started to dance like a man possessed with boundless energy. The onlookers stood there transfixed they'd obviously never seen dancing of such a high standard before. This man was in a class of his own and was using a method taught by very talented instructors, it was certainly a performance worth watching and they all stood open mouthed hardly daring to breathe.

As Ivan finished the watching dancers and the producer clapped him vigorously for quite some time, they were all obviously very impressed. Bowing humbly, his face smiling, he then waited for the producer to comment. There then followed a meeting in a small office at the front of the theatre between the manager, the interpreter, and a very nervous Ivan. The manager had a problem on his hands as money was short that season, and most of the regular troupe had already agreed to work for slightly less money. He was worried that to offer Ivan too little he might lose him, perhaps to a Paris Theatre, so he started to question him most cautiously. He started slowly just to make sure he wasn't misunderstood in any way.

'Are you free to work with us at the moment?'

Ivan nodded when he heard the question.

'Yes I am.'

'Good! And what sort of money are you expecting?'

Ivan wasn't really ready for this this, he'd never been paid to dance in a large theatre before, and had no real expectations of long term work.

'Whatever you are willing to give me for what I'm worth.'

The Manager looked puzzled. Good dancers were usually more positive about money, perhaps the man had been out of work for quite a while and might be glad to start again for a small amount.

'Before I decide on engaging you I'd like to see you perform for just a bit longer. Can you come back again about this time tomorrow?'
Ivan smiled and nodded not believing his luck. 'Yes of course. And can I bring my wife?'

'Yes of course you can. And does she also dance?' Ivan shook his head.

'No only when we are at a party.'

The manager paused a moment. 'There will be a few quite important people here then some of them are helping finance our season here. Thank you for coming, you are just the sort of dancer that we are looking for, we'll hopefully see you tomorrow then."

The manager then stood up and held out his hand. Ivan shook it and nodding to the interpreter left the room with a look of relief on his face. This was indeed a good day in his life now perhaps he could at least fulfill his life's ambition to be an outstanding dancer, his family were going to be more than surprised at his afternoons adventure.

During his walk back to the camp on the outskirts of town his mind was buzzing with thoughts of the following day, would he be up to giving the right sort of performance to clinch the job he certainly hoped so.

On his arrival back at the camp Petra and the children were preparing supper and she seemed surprised that he'd been gone so long.

'Did you have a good walk Ivan? You seem to have been out ages.'
Ivan smiled and took off his coat.

'Yes I have and guess what's happened?' He said.

Petra shook her head. 'No tell me.'

'I think I've got a dancing job. Not just for a night but the whole season at the town theatre called the Arsenal, and it's a huge place seating thousands.'

Petra looked at him in disbelief. 'And are they really going to pay you to dance there?' Ivan nodded and hugged her vigorously.

'Yes. That is if I dance well for them tomorrow at an audition. And you can come and watch as well, that's if you want to?'

Petra stood there in amazement and it was quite a few seconds before she could reply. 'That's fantastic. Of course I'll come with you.'

Ivan certainly looked more relaxed than he'd been for quite some time, at last he could see a better future for himself and his family providing he could pass the audition the next day. Now he could tell his relations that with luck tomorrow at least they could eat reasonably well for the next few months.

The following day he arrived at the theatre much earlier than the other dancers but fortunately the manager was already there, and seemed please that he was at least on time. He introduced himself as Francois to Petra and asked Ivan to start getting ready he said the other members of the committee would be along shortly. Ivan calmly left and went backstage to change knowing that he was going to give one of the best performances of his life at least he hoped so. Petra sat next to Francois and used the little French that she'd learned at school all those years ago, it seemed to work and they got on very well together until the other committee members arrived.

When everyone was seated Francois signaled that Ivan could start and all eyes turned towards the stage that was at that point unlit by spotlights. Ivan glanced out over the heads of the few people present and imagined that the theatre was packed with people and he was going to dance for a first night a new ballet, one that had never been seen before. He nervously moved forward towards the front of the stage and as the music started he

32

went into a slow routine. This lasted about five minutes then as the music speeded up he started to perform steps that he'd learned way back at the Mariinski school. His adaptation of this part had taken him many weeks to perfect and he'd never forgotten them as difficult as they were.

The onlookers sat there entranced unable to believe their eyes, this was an absolutely spectacular performance from a man well past his youth. What they didn't know was that almost from the minute Ivan started to dance a bee had settled on his arm and to try and get rid of it he danced and waved his arms around furiously to shake it off. The more he moved the louder it buzzed, until finally it decided to move on. Ivan went on dancing for at least fifteen minutes until the music came to an end where he bowed gracefully and smiling went to leave the stage. All those watching stood and clapped him and the manager Francois knew by their faces that he had indeed a winner on his hands, all that was left now was to negotiate a contract with Ivan that would be suitable for the coming season.

After conferring at length with the committee members Francoise went backstage to talk to Ivan this was certainly a very lucky find on his part. This dancer certainly knew his stuff and was streets ahead of all the French ones, the method of teaching in Russia must be of a very high standard indeed.

Once back in the dressing room together with the help of an interpreter Francois went through the formalities of agreeing a salary with Ivan, and getting him to sign the contract papers. Ivan asked if he knew of any cheap suitable lodgings in the area and Francois said he'd enquire about them for him. Ivan was impressed with the way things had gone for him and couldn't wait to tell Petra the outcome of the audition, although he felt that she must somehow know by the reaction of the committee that he'd made it. They went back into the theatre past the stage which by now was filling up with dancers and crew. The committee welcomed Ivan and congratulated him on his appointment to the cast, then Francois asked him to attend the following morning for his first rehearsal session.

On leaving the theatre Ivan took Petra to a nearby café to celebrate and tell her the good news which she had already guessed, and about the problem with the bee. This funny story and the vodkas they consumed made her very much happier than she'd been for many years. Now perhaps they could start to plan a better future with fewer problems than they had encountered in the past in Russia.

Chapter Ten

The New Home

True to his word Francois found Ivan a small place on the outskirts of town to rent quite cheaply, and with the purchase of a few bits of furniture soon had the place very comfy. As a bonus it had a large barn outbuilding close by. With a few alterations it had enough room to house the remaining family as well. This was an extra benefit for them all as now they could be together in reasonable comfort, plus with the addition of a few animals they could become almost self sufficient. It wasn't until Ivan received his first payment at the end of the first month's rehearsal, that it dawned on them how rich they now were in comparison to their lives in Russia. Not only could they eat better there was money left over for luxuries they'd never been able to afford before. The children's lives were changed completely by their new life and from dawn to dusk they were kept busy with the animals, gathering fuel for the fires and fetching water from the well. This was the first time any of them had even seen real soap sold in a shop. The peasants in Russia had always made their own from animal fats. All the children now wanted to help with the washing and making bubbles this to them was great fun indeed.

When the time came for the opening night at the theatre the whole family were given free tickets for the great and exiting occasion, this meant dressing up in the best clothes that they could muster. The whole place was packed and every seat sold out weeks before and there was an air of terrific excitement everywhere, and even the most expensive boxes were all taken.

As the curtain rose a hush came over the audience then the stage lights revealed the lavish set before the first dancers appeared on stage. It was almost fifteen minutes before Ivan made his first appearance, his dancing was as dramatic as ever and this was clapped vigorously by the audience. He had one of the premier parts and by the end of the night the audience stood and applauded long and loud each time he took a curtain call. It was one of the most satisfying nights of his life and by the time he reached his dressing room there was a large crowd waiting for his autograph, and to congratulate him on his marvelous performance.

Francois was also there beaming and well satisfied that his discovery had reached his expectations and was on the way to becoming a star performer in his own right. When finally left alone in the dressing room Francois turned to Ivan and managed to convey his congratulations on the night's performance, despite the language difference between them. When Ivan finally changed and reached the main entrance all the family were waiting to greet him, especially the children who were thrilled to be part of it all. Anna the eldest daughter was bubbling with excitement and really showed it. 'You were fantastic Daddy and everybody loved your dancing, that was the best you've ever performed.'

'Thank you Anna. I really felt good tonight let's hope the rest of the season goes as well and the audiences fill the place just like tonight.'

Well it did go well and throughout the season Ivan got better and fitter all the time and the theatre did far more business than it had done for many years. His brother also seemed to fit in well and worked almost non-stop throughout the year, and so by the end of it they had all saved enough money to last through the winter. The children were by then almost word perfect in French and spent many happy hours passing this on to their parents. Life seemed so much better in France and each day they discovered different things of interest in the town and the surrounding area.

The winter that followed was cold and wet so not much exiting happened until the spring when the whole town came alive again with religious festivals and carnivals. The following season was just as successful for the family as a whole and for Ivan at the theatre which did fantastic business most of the year with several new productions. So well that most of the building received a face-lift after the last show ended.

It was in late February of 1909 that a famous Russian ballet Producer first got news of the high standard of dancing at the Arsenal Theatre, and travelled from Paris to watch a performance there. His name was Sergei Diaghilev and he was in the process of moving a company to Paris from Russia called the Ballets Russes, to which he had already signed Ida Rubenstein, and Anna Pavlova together with Vaslav Nijinsky. So impressed was he at the performances of some of the dancers there that he signed two of them at once, one being Ivan. The fact that they were also of Russian origin really clinched it for him. They both helped solve a problem he was having bringing lesser known dancers out of Russia due to contractual problems with the Maryinsky management. The money he offered them both was slightly more than what they were earning, he also paid the Arsenal Theatre a small fee for terminating both their contracts. He promised to get one of the theatre assistants to meet them at the Paris Station to take them to their apartment which would be reasonably close to the Theatre. Ivan just couldn't believe his luck and to be dancing in the same company as Pavlova and Nijinsky was incredible in itself. To him Ivan an unknown dancer this was like a dream.

Born in 1878 and now at the age of thirty he was no spring chicken, he wondered just how long his fitness would last perhaps another ten years if he looked after himself. He'd last seen the young Pavlova, who was now a star, way back in 1891 at the Mariinsky Ballet School when he was just thirteen years old. He wondered what she'd look like now and also if she'd remember him probably not, it seemed almost a lifetime ago.

His brother was happy for him that he'd managed to get such a wonderful job with the Paris Ballet Russes Company, but after long discussions decided to stay on where they were for a bit longer. Moving to such a large place really didn't appeal to them at all, they were content just as they were. Now they could spread out a bit with the use of another building between them, and also it would be a small problem getting rid of the animals they'd acquired. The furniture such as it was Ivan decided to leave there and get some more in Paris.

The brother being a peasant farmer at heart didn't think that Paris was suitable for them but perhaps maybe if Ivan found it to his liking they just might change their minds and join him. In the last month before leaving Ivan spent some time packing and the odd hour or two with the other dancers rehearsing at the theatre. They had found by this time a replacement for him so he didn't feel a bit guilty at leaving, the new man seemed quite capable and fitted in well with the others. Francois spoke to him a few days before he left and wished him well and said he was looking forward to seeing him dance in the Paris production.

On the day of the family's departure all the others were there to see them off at the station, this was to be their first time on a train and a new experience for them all. They never could afford such a luxury as this before. Their only sight of trains had been from the outside of the station and meant only for the very rich to use. This was going to be a memorable experience for them all in more ways than one and once on board Petra was to make a statement that Ivan wasn't quite expecting. She waited until the children were all settled in the corner of the carriage before speaking quietly.

'Ivan I've got something very important to tell you.'

Ivan looked at her wondering just what she could possibly be going to say at a time like this.

'Well what is it Petra ?'

'I'm pregnant. That is I think so.'
Ivan smiled and hugged her. No wonder she'd looked so radiant the last few days he thought that it was the thought of going to Paris .'Why didn't you mention it sooner? I could have told the rest of the family.

'I wasn't sure and anyway we can let them all know when it happens.' This was the icing on the cake thought Ivan but with another mouth to feed he hoped his new job would work out for the better. Anyway he would have a whole season under his belt before the happy day arrived. As the train chugged on they both fell asleep happy beyond belief that things were certainly now looking rosy for all of them.

Chapter Eleven

Paris

As the train pulled slowly into the suburbs of Paris they all sat open mouthed looking at the thousands of houses that flashed by before the huge blocks of flats near the centre came into view. This was a huge city, far bigger than any place that they'd been to before, and Ivan began to have doubts as to whether they'd be able to afford to live there. As the train hissed to a halt all the passengers rushed off hurriedly and Ivan's family nervously followed them all with their many suitcases and bags. Just outside the barrier a smartly dressed man approached them holding their name written on a piece of cardboard, Ivan smiled at him and nodded. With the few words of French that Ivan had by now acquired he managed with the help of the children to let the man whose name was René know that they were the family he was waiting for.

Outside the station, having boarded a large motor bus, Réné paid the conductor the fares to their destination. At the end of their journey they all got off the bus and followed René to an apartment block within a dark courtyard, where he stopped inside to talk to an old squeaky voiced old woman who seemed to be in charge. She took a bunch of keys off the hook in her office marked "Concierge" and led them up a dark staircase to a flat on the second floor. As she opened the flat door she muttered something in French then handed Ivan the keys and departed.

René followed them around as they all inspected the apartment it seemed as though it had been empty for quite some time and smelt very musty, and when they had looked at all the rooms he waited for their comments and approval.

'Very nice!' Said Petra smiling. 'At least that is when we've tidied it up a bit.' René edged uncomfortably towards the door then took an envelope from his pocket and handed it to Ivan. The Producer told me to give you this Monsieur it's your instructions for tomorrow.'

Ivan took the envelope from him and thanked him for escorting them and the man left closing the door behind him.

Petra looked at Ivan and glanced at the envelope waiting for him to open it. He sensed her natural curiosity and smiled as he tore it open, his face changed a little and he looked a bit more serious as he read it.

'Well! What does he say then?' Said Petra.

Ivan paused and glanced at the letter again before answering.

'Just that I'm to report to the Theatre du Chatelet tomorrow morning for rehearsal at ten with my shoes and tights. The theatre has been changed from the Opera Theatre for some reason and he's given me a map showing how to get there. After the first rehearsal with the choreographer the Producer is going to tell us the programme for the first season. He has also paid our rent for the first month here and will take it out of my wages.'

Petra looked a little relieved she was half expecting something was wrong, that the show might not happen, and they might have to find some other work. 'That's good news! So now we'd better see what we need in the flat, there doesn't seem to be much furniture in here.'

As they walked around the small dark flat they found only two small wooden beds, an old dusty wardrobe and a few kitchen utensils next to an old earthenware sink with a dripping brass tap and a fat covered old gas oven. This to them was a luxury after collecting water from the well for years. On the walls hung strange crude looking paintings as though the artist had departed hurriedly without them and probably unable to pay the rent. The whole place was cold and damp with cobwebs everywhere and the smell was overpowering, enough to persuade Petra to open two of the windows despite the cold air outside. Turning to Ivan she made for her bag and took out a pencil and paper.

'We'd better make a note of the things we need for tonight then I'll do a proper shopping tomorrow when you go to rehearsal, Ivan.'

After making a list they locked the flat and made their way downstairs and into the bustling streets of Montmarte to the nearest market the noise of the crowds there was deafening.They managed to find almost everything they needed to make themselves comfortable for a few nights. It didn't take them long to find out that they were now living among hundreds of struggling artists and entertainers, the way they were dressed said it all. The children thought this first visit to a Paris market was most exiting and Petra made sure they both held her hand moving between so many people.

On return to their new flat they caught sight of the Concierge peering out of her makeshift office at them as they crossed the courtyard, she certainly made sure nobody entered without her knowledge. She gave the impression of being a rather sad and lonely old woman dressed entirely in black. Once back in the apartment they made the place quite comfortable within hours and Petra then got a nice meal ready for them. After which children Anna and Mika spent a lot of their time just looking out of the various windows at the other flats opposite, also at the traffic and people in the street below. During the evening the flat was reasonably warm and after the children had been bedded down Petra made up a bed of sorts on the floor in the other room. This didn't bother them too much as soon they'd be able to afford another proper bed with Ivan's wages.

The following morning Ivan noticed the frost that had formed on the roofs outside, and ice starting to appear on the inside corners of the bedroom window. This in itself didn't bother him as the winters in Russia had been much worse and they'd become used to them in time.
When Ivan left the flat at just before eight o'clock he'd already decided to find a bus going the best part of the way to the theatre, just to save his energy for the rehearsal. He'd already worked out that the distance was about ten kilometres and that to walk it would probably take about one and a half hours. This proved to be the right decision even though the wait for the bus was quite a long one, but he still got to the theatre very much earlier than most of the others.

A few minutes after ten the dancers were all dressed and assembled in the front seats at the theatre as the Producer arrived with the choreographer whom he introduced as Mikhail Fokine, together with a young shy looking music composer called Igor Stravinski. He explained that the type of performance that they would be expected to give would be groundbreaking and never been seen before anywhere else. The reason for the change of theatre was that two of the sponsors had withdrawn at the last minute and the first theatre had been booked. He then went on to introduce the dancers one at a time starting with Ida Rubenstein Vaslav Nijinski and Tamara Karsavina until he got to Anna Pavlova. Ivan looked at her in surprise, she certainly looked different from when he'd last seen her. She looked absolutely radiant and full of energy he couldn't wait to see her dance again.

When it finally came to his introduction by Diaghilev the rest of the cast looked at Ivan wondering who he was and the reason for his inclusion in the cast, to most of them he was an unknown.

He pointed to Ivan 'Now we come to a dancer whose name is Ivan and has been recommended by several people in France and Russia to me, and I've also seen him perform in another part of France. He was originally in your company in St Petersburg many years ago but left through lack of sponsorship. Since then he has performed quite regularly at quite important events and fairs dancing in the style that we are going to use very soon. He has perfected a stylish gypsy method of his own and that together with Mikhail will take you all through this kind of routine ready for our next production.'

Mikhail nodded he had already been briefed about this beforehand the others looked a little perplexed as they were already stars in their own right, and were used to being consulted on radical changes like this to their routine well in advance. The producer then went on with his instructions.

'For those of you still under contract with the Mariinski Theatre your future is assured for the next few years by the State, but for newcomers I will personally guarantee your salaries and accommodation for the next two years unless you seriously break your contract in any way." He then moved towards the centre seats and motioned Mikhail to take over the first rehearsal who then mounted the stage to speak.

'First of all for the few of you that have never met me I am first and foremost a dancer and always will be but at the moment have been chosen to be your Choreographer. So from now on you will be accountable to me during your working hours, and you will find me I hope a fair but thorough person. It will be long hours until opening night but it will all be worth the effort in the end I hope. You are some of the best dancers in the world and we expect to get a first class performance from you during the run of this production. Thank you all for your attention we will now start this rehearsal.'

He then called Ivan to centre stage and then asked him to give a very brief demonstration of his own dancing. Ivan looked at him standing there and studied briefly the shape of his body, it was painfully thin but the muscles in the thighs and upper arm showed that he was indeed a very fit man. Mikhail stood back and watched as Ivan went through his short routine the others looked on with interest it was a type of dancing that most of them had never seen before.

After Ivan had finished Mikael followed with a close repeat of the dance and asked each of the others to do the same. Of course none of them came close to Ivan's showing with the exception of Nijinski who really excelled himself, at the end of his fantastic dance during which he appeared to almost have wires attached to him he leaped higher than all the rest. They all stood there and applauded loudly. Nijinski modestly bowed and smiled with satisfaction he'd certainly made it look easy and Mikael knew at this moment he had the right cast for the show, all he had to do was lick them into shape in the few remaining weeks left.

The remainder of the first day went well and by the end of it both Mikhael and Diaghilev were well pleased with the result and all the dancers seemed to be enjoying this new experience tremendously. Even the terrible noise of the carpenters and stage-hands making and moving sets around didn't seem to distract them too much, and it certainly could have been most off putting at times. The only one who was slightly dissatisfied was Ida Rubenstein she wondered why she had to go through this change of routine as her first role didn't involve this type of dancing. Mikhael pointed out to her that it was essential that they were all going to be involved in it at some point during the next few seasons, and he wouldn't take any excuses for them not knowing the steps. This answer seemed to satisfy her and she was soon smiling again, Nijinski came to the end of the session resolved to take very little part in the rest of the rehearsal sessions and just do his own thing. He figured that he normally rehearsed and danced at three times the speed of the others and didn't want to waste time working at their pace.

The following weeks of rehearsal went well and the dancers really got on together apart from a few differences between Nijinski and Mikhael Fokine. Ivan was slightly embarrassed that his kind of routine should be used to spark off the performances of such famous dancers, but he and the others soon came to terms with the situation. In the final two weeks before opening night the whole theatre was in chaos because the space usually reserved for the orchestra was found to be too small and unsuitable. The unusual step of removing the first two rows of seats and the addition of new orchestra seating changed the whole look of the Auditorium. Diaghilev took it upon himself to order the redecoration of large parts of the theatre to enhance the feel of the place despite being supposedly short of money. There were whispers around the cast that Nijinski had moved out of his small hotel and was sharing Diaghilev's more sumptuous apartment, but the dancers seemed to think this unimportant. There had been bigger problems in St Petersburg before the cast had moved to Paris mostly financial and who was playing what part.

All over Paris large posters from a drawing of Karsavina by Valentin Svetlov were appearing announcing the Ballet Russes season it was at that time the most publicized event of the year.

Ivan and his family were getting quite settled in to their new home in Montmarte and had acquired enough furniture to make themselves comfortable. The nearby markets were a bonus and much cheaper than the more central parts of Paris. Both the children were now well settled in at school, and Mikael now six years old was already beginning to show an artistic streak. The whole family would visit the museums and art galleries whenever possible and Mikael would sit for quite some time doing rough sketches of religious works of art.

On Sundays they would all go to church and he would always try to sit near stained glass windows whenever possible. Anna was by now eleven years old and showing an interest in dress design. She spent a lot of time with her mother making clothes for herself. This pastime was one her mother really encouraged her in and the nearby market stalls were her main suppliers, even the smallest scraps of cheap material were not ignored.

Petra now with a little time on her hands had taken on a part time teaching job at a private college nearby to coach diplomats in basic Russian. This little job came in handy for the extra money for special treats for the family. The information that was being passed on to her by some of the minor diplomats regarding tragic events back in Russia made her sad indeed at times, and she hoped that the relations they'd left behind there were safe and well. She was thankful that her family had left the country when they had. By now she was beginning to swell a bit, she wondered how long it would be before she'd be forced to stop working. Now that Ivan was getting a regular wage perhaps things would be better for them.

Chapter Twelve

Opening Night

When at last the night finally arrived for the Premiere of Le Pavillon d'Armide and first of the many productions of the 1909 Paris Ballet Russes season, almost everyone connected to the arts and theatre were there. Such notables as Isadora Duncan, Auguste Rodin, Yvette Gillbert, Claud Debussy, Maurice Ravel, and Jean Cocteau, were present. In the boxes were the Russian Ambassador, the French Foreign Minister, representatives of the Monte Carlo Opera, and the Metropolitan Opera House, New York. Scattered around the dress circle were the most beautiful female members of the Opera and the Comédie-Francaise.

Backstage Nijinski had spent half an hour warming up in his old clothes then took another half hour to change and make up. When he had finally finished the transformation was stunning, he was another person indeed the Favorite Slave of the Princess Armida. The opening scene with Karsavina and Alexandra Baldina was joined by Nijinski dressed in a multi coloured top embellished with lots of silk, and ermine, a wired skirt and knee breeches and garters. The three of them danced with such passion and quality that seemed to stun the audience, they had not seen this kind of Russian dancing in their lives before.

At the end of this piece and as the two female dancers left the stage Nijinski moved quickly towards the edge of the stage and took a massive leap into the wings. The audience gasped at this audacious leap not knowing that this was not part of the planned choreography, and was a last minute decision by him. The rest of the performance was just as magical with solo performances most riveting right to the last moments. Although some who watched the previews thought the programme a bit of a mish mash, on the night it all came together very well. A last minute insertion of the Tchaikowsky/Petipa 'Bluebird' variation danced by Nijiinski and Karsavina was magical to watch. She followed this later with some strange Russian character-dancing, followed by The dance of the warriors with Adolph Bolm leading. Together with the erotic female dances led by Fedorova. The superb costumes designed by Léon Baskt especially Ida Rubenstein's in Cléopatrá, were the cream on the cake that night and they were absolutely stunning as was her performance. After the final curtain Nijinski was cheered and clapped all the way to his dressing room, he was now the king of ballet indeed. The huge orchestra just gave up playing the closing notes unable to hear themselves owing to the noise of the audience's cheers.

Ivan once back in his dressing room like the rest of the cast knew that it was really a team performance, and that each and every one of them had contributed to make it a night to remember. He wondered what his tutor would have thought of his dancing now after all these years, he'd certainly come a long way since then. He knew that he'd never make it as a star performer but to be dancing in this company was satisfaction and an achievement in itself, and at least it would keep him employed for at least two years. He felt satisfied that at least he'd made a contribution to some parts of the programme with his interpretation of Russian folk dancing. For those of the audience who made it to the dancers dressing rooms there was a crush to get autographs signed, the rest just crowded the bars and seemed unwilling to leave the theatre. And it was well after midnight that the last ones left some of them just didn't want to go home at all.

The following morning after the late night celebration party for the cast at the theatre, the daily French newspapers had bold headlines praising the previous nights performance. And in them Nijinski was hailed as God of the dance for his magical leaps and pirouettes the likes of which they had never witnessed before. As each national and international newspaper became available the impact of the their first nights performance made the cast and production team realize that they had possibly achieved a special place in ballet history.

Both Diaghilev and Fokine were kept busy in the office answering calls from the press and representatives of other national theatres who were anxiously trying to book them for the following season. They now at last had the promise of the Paris Opera House for the following year's season, and had to sort that out first. It obviously meant trying to plan a completely new programme and this meant more rehearsals for the company with Scheherazade and Les Sylphides as the main attractions and this entailed completely new sets and musical scores.

During the closing weeks of the first season things went well for the company and even the most humble dancers of the group including Ivan were now being recognized daily in the streets. It made them all feel slightly more important than when they'd first arrived in Paris.

Meanwhile Petra had purchased copies of the newspapers with the best notices of the ballet and started a scrapbook with the children of Ivan's dancing achievements. Little did they dream of what lay in store for him during the coming years. Just as a treat Petra would take the children occasionally on a walk to see the crowds arriving by large motor cars at the theatre for that nights performance. During the daytime after school and at week-ends Petra would take the children on long walks around Paris explaining the history of the city. Ivan would sleep until late morning usually to save his energy for the nightly performance.

Ivan was slightly nervous about dancing at the Opera House which he had been told was a very much larger theatre so he went to look at it one morning before work. It really took his breath away and to even walk around the place took almost ten minutes whilst avoiding the traffic and the hordes of tourists and artists sketching the building.

At the end of the second season which was sold out from start to finish the last night's programme was extended to include Ida Rubenstein dancing Salomé. This additional piece was so well received that it was decided the following day to include it in the forthcoming Opera House programme. Some days later Nijinski with Diaghilev left for London to check out the suitable theatres there with a view to taking the company there for their possible appearance late the following year. Their next move was for the whole contracted company to return to St Petersburg for a few performances in September, Ivan, although not being one of the Marinski contracted group also went with them. The sponsors of the Russian visit insisted that all the national dancers must be included At this point Nijinski caught a bug from possibly drinking the Paris water and was laid low in Paris for over a month thereby missing the St Petersburg performances.

And so ended a very exciting enjoyable and different French season for Ivan and his family, this was definitely a year to remember.

Just weeks before Ivan left for St Petersburg their next child Boris was born and the family was now six. This child was their first one born outside Russia and they hoped to have many more God willing. The trip back to St Petersburg was the first time Ivan had been separated from Petra since they'd married all those years ago, and from the time the family had tearfully seen him off at the station he'd felt very alone despite being in a carriage-full of dancers.

Once back in St Petersburg a lot of the cast were disgruntled about their allocation of accommodation and complained to the management about it. To Ivan his small hotel room seemed quite adequate and the food although slightly different from what he was accustomed to it was satisfactory. And anyway it was only for a few weeks, then he'd be back to Petra's wonderful food again. The rehearsals were a bit spasmodic owing to Nijinski being late most mornings, despite many warnings by the management and of fines by them. He seemed to lose interest in proceedings at times and of course those who'd read of the casts successes in Paris thought it had gone to his head a bit and he was getting slightly careless.

Nijinski seemed unimpressed with the Maryinski style of presentation and couldn't bring himself to focus on the rehearsals at all, he felt he had more to offer doing it his way. He thought that the programme was too traditional and uninspiring. The problem that beset the company was that the decision to put on Giselle was disputed by Pavlova, who didn't want to be upstaged by Nijiinski in the premier role. She thought and rightly so that he'd had enough praise heaped upon him in Paris and didn't think he warranted it. When things finally came to a head she reluctantly withdrew from the part. Nijiinski despite this then went on to dance superbly as Albrecht which ballet lovers talked about for many years.

Ivan really enjoyed being part of the company back in his own country and felt safe amidst townspeople away from the troubles of the farming community. He wrote to Petra and the children almost daily about the life of himself and the people of St Petersburg, it was a city he'd only read about in the past and he was amazed at the size of it. He spent many hours when not working visiting the many museums and churches in the city and making notes to be able to tell the family about it all when he returned to Paris. During his stay he made friends with quite a lot of people from the audience who'd followed his career with interest through the past years. He was approached at one point by a member of the Marynski Board and asked whether he'd like to finish his remaining graduate time with them. He turned out to be one of the directors but Ivan politely refused saying that he felt a little old for such a move, and didn't want to disrupt his family in Paris as they were settled there comfortably.

Chapter Thirteen

The Second Season

The year started with rehearsals for the second season of the Ballet Russes at the Paris Opera House in late March, after a winter of problems for the company's winter season at St Petersburg. It was going to take some sorting out by Diagilev as some of the lead dancers were now much less than enthusiastic about their roles. One who was in a more positive mood and really bursting with energy was Ida Rubenstein down to dance in Schéhérazade written by Alexandre Benois, this was to be the most testing part of her career so far. The costumes for this season were to be designed once again by Léon Baskt and the music by composer Rimsky-Korsakov. The interruption to their Paris routine mainly brought about by the very strict St Petersburg artistry took some getting back, and it was quite some days before they'd all settled down again. In St Petersburg Pavlova had already performed in the Marynski production with the resident group and had really excelled herself in the Giselle role.

This was watched by promoters from London and led to her withdrawal from the Paris season and her signing a contract for the London Palace Theatre. This was a blow to Diagilev as Karsavina had already signed another contract to appear at the London Colliseum. This just left him with Ida Rubenstein as a lead dancer and he just prayed that she didn't catch something, there would certainly be nobody to replace her. And to add to choreographer Fokine's problems a few French dancers had to be added to the cast at the last moment and he didn't speak good enough French. There were also problems concerning the rights of the Rimski-Korsakov music for Shéhérazade but this was resolved before rehearsals got under way. This was designed to be the main attraction to follow on from small set pieces from Le Festin, Prince Igor, and Carnaval.

A lot of time and effort went into the rehearsal for this programme and the sets and costumes once again designed by Léon Bakst were absolutely stunning, so much so that word got round the artistic world and all of the seats were sold out long before opening night arrived. Among many notable artists in the audience for the first night when it finally arrived was Marc Chagall, Pablo Picasso, millionaire Walter Guinness, and actress Sarah Bernhardt. When the curtain went up on the Schéhérazade part of the programme the audience sat there open mouthed at the sight of the sets and costumes, the like of which had never been seen before. Ida Rubenstein was sensational as Zobeida, and Nijinski as the Golden Slave danced the greatest role of his life a repeat of this kind of performance has yet to be seen.

So revolutionary was the whole experience of that night that a whole new artistic trend was established throughout Europe, with fabrics, jewelry, and clothing loosely based on the designs seen on stage that night. Such exotic and near pornographic performance by the two was the talk of the town in the following weeks.

When the curtain finally came down there was a mad rush to the artists changing rooms for congratulations and autographs, after this had subsided the wealthy and titled patrons followed to shower their praises on the dancers.

Ivan sitting quietly in his own dressing room he shared with two others was surprised to see a smiling Leon Bakst enter followed by a much younger man.

'Well done Ivan! You danced superbly tonight, I would like to introduce you to a friend of mine who is very interested in your dancing. This is Marc Chagal and a pupil at an art school I run. He'd like to speak to you a few moments if you can spare the time, I've got to talk to some of the others so I'll leave you a few minutes together.' Bakst then left the room.

Ivan nodded wondering what the man wanted, dance fans generally just wanted him to sign their programme for them, this was very unusual. The man moved closer to his chair before speaking in Russian.

'I have been watching you dance for quite a few performances now and admire you tremendously and wondered if you would perhaps help me?' Ivan looked at the man quizzically.

'Help you! In what way?'

'Well you see I'm an artist and I'd very much like you to pose for me, that's of course if you're not too busy. You have a wonderful body and I'd very much like to paint you, of course I'll pay whatever is reasonable.' Ivan thought for a moment before answering. "Yes that will be alright providing the management agree to me doing it.'

'I'm sure it will be, Leon checked that before bringing me to see you and I have painted the company's dancers before In St Petersburg.' Over the man's shoulder Ivan spotted his two companions grinning. They obviously thought Ivan was going to be more than an artists sitter. He ignored them and shook Chagall's hand warmly.

'Let me know when you want me to start. How do you want me to dress for the job?'

'Just as you are now will do. Here's where I'm staying.' He passed Ivan a small card. "Perhaps tomorrow if you can make it?' Ivan took the card and glanced at it noting it was one of the streets near his apartment.

'I'll try and make it straight after lunch tomorrow.' Ivan replied.

'Excellent I look forward to seeing you.'

Chagall then left the room leaving Ivan slightly puzzled as to why anyone should want to think about painting him, he was no different to any other dancers in the group. Perhaps he was one of those strange men he'd read about in books. Who knows? Petra would certainly have something to say about it when he told her later.

The following day Ivan arrived at Chagall's apartment slightly apprehensive and not knowing what was expected of him. The door was opened by a much younger man who led him upstairs to the top floor, where Chagall was waiting to greet him. The room itself was bathed in sunshine with large windows not only on every wall but from the huge skylights above. Ivan had never seen such a place before this man must surely be quite rich he thought.

The next few hours went quite quickly and although he'd never had to sit still for such a long time Ivan thought this was indeed an easy way to earn a living. Much better than having to rehearse and dance the way he did. At the end of the session Ivan casually glanced at the canvas on his way out, he was astonished to find that what Chagall had spent all afternoon working on just didn't make sense to him at all. This kind of painting was new to him in all respects not the sort of portrait that hung in the galleries around Paris, they at least made sense to him, this was something quite different. No doubt the man probably knew what he was doing and maybe this was some modern method that he'd not heard about but it was certainly different from anything he'd ever seen. It did seem odd that someone should be prepared to pay him to sit still and paint something as odd as that, surely nobody would be interested in such a weird painting.

Later that afternoon being quizzed by the children about his new job they were eager to know just what it was like. Leading with the questions was Anna keen to be the first to find out all about it.

'What was it you had to do father? Did you have to take your clothes off?'

Ivan smiled and shook his head. 'No it wasn't that sort of session. I just kept my stage clothes on that's all.'

'And was he a real painter then?' Said Nika."

Ivan nodded. 'Of course he was. And a fairly famous one too.'

Young Mikael looking serious not wanting to be left out of this dicussion chipped in next with what he thought was a really grown up question.

'But he hasn't left any paint on you father, or have you washed it of already.'

Ivan laughed at this remark. 'No Mikael he just painted my picture on some canvas that's all.'

Petra who had present watching all this seemed very amused at the children's natural curiosity and waited for a lull in the questions to ask

54

some herself.

'How long will he take to do it then Ivan?'

'I don't know Petra maybe three or four sittings. Who knows?'

'And was it hard for you sitting still for so long?' Said Petra.

'Not really. He didn't mind me moving occasionally, it wasn't too difficult.'

Mikael wasn't satisfied with this explanation and decided to ask another question.

'Surely you don't get paid for just sitting down do you?'
Ivan shook his head. "No sometimes he asks me to stand up for a few minutes for a change.'

Petra decided that it was time to call a halt to the questions she glanced at Boris it was a good job he wasn't old enough to join in.

'That's enough now you father needs to get ready for the theatre now and he needs to eat as well. So go into the other room and play for a while.'

Later that night Leon Bakst told the company that the next production would include Gisselle and that it might just be one of the most difficult programmes they would work on. Rehearsals were to start in the next few days and Karsavina had been released from her London contract for one month to dance the lead in it.

She did not however turn up at rehearsal until the third day and by this time Nijinski was proving more awkward than usual. and it took quite some time to placate him. He seemed unable at times to lift Karsavina high enough owing to his size in comparison to hers. It took many days for him to master the lift but he more than made up for this in his interpretation of Albrecht which was superb.

The first night of Giselle was greeted with rapturous applause by the audience. Colonel Teliakovsky of the Marynski board who had travelled from Russia to attend the performance told them afterwards that he wanted them all in St Petersburg in the autumn with Pavlova in the lead.

Such was the popularity of this Paris season that it was extended a few weeks before their visit to Brussels for two performances of Prince Igor. The full cast was used this time including Ivan who really enjoyed the trip immensely despite the weather being a lot colder.

And so ended another successful season for the company but some of the members of the Marynski board of directors were either envious or disapproved of their European success and wanted to stop financing them. After a lot of heated discussion Diaghilev decided to break away on his own and to finance the company by other means. This meant reducing the cast quite a lot and taking on local cheaper dancers, one of the first to be notified was unfortunately Ivan. After being informed of the cuts Ivan left for home worried about his future and the thought of having to tell Petra.

Back in the flat and alone with his wife he began to relate all that had happened that day.

'It's been a bad day for us Petra I've lost my job at the theatre. So have a few of the others. They are having to cut costs as St Petersburg has stopped all the funds.'

Petra looked at him in dismay hardly believing what she was hearing.

'How are we going to manage then Ivan, we can't live on my wages?' Ivan put his arms around her and drew her close.

'It's not quite that bad really. Diaghilev has promised to pay the next months rent for us and there are two more well known artists wanting me to sit for them on a regular basis. That will help until I can find another job of some sort.'

Tears were slowly trickling down Petra's sad face but by the time Ivan had finished she had recovered a bit.

'Perhaps I can work a few more hours each week, that's if they'll let me and I can find someone to mind Boris on the days that you are working.'

Ivan shook his head. 'That won't be necessary my love we have managed before on much less money, things will turn out alright you'll see.'

The following day Ivan returned to the theatre for his things and final wages. Diaghilev was in the office and sat there glum faced worried that he'd possibly done the wrong thing in breaking away from the St Petersburg financial set-up. It was a hard decision to get rid of some of the group especially Ivan whom he thought a lot of throughout the past two seasons. He motioned him to sit on the chair facing him.

'Thank you for coming in Ivan, I wanted to tell you how much you've been appreciated by everyone here. Your dancing has been first class on every occasion and you've never once complained unlike some.'

'Thank you sir.' Replied Ivan. 'You have been most kind to me at all times.'

Diaghilev paused a moment. "What are your plans for the immediate future Ivan?'

'Just a few sittings a week for local artists that's all.'

'Is that enough to live on?' Said Diaghilev. 'Would you like me to give your name to the people running the next production here at this theatre. They are probably short of good all round dancers?'
Ivan then smiled for the first time that day. 'Yes thanks that would be helpful even for a few days occasionally.' Diaghilev then picked up an envelope from his desk and passed it to Ivan.

'I've put the rent money and a little extra in with your wages as token of our appreciation, do drop in whenever you're passing you will always be welcome here.'

He then stood up and shook Ivan's hand warmly. This was indeed one of the hard parts of being a producer, he knew that he would probably never come across such a naturally talented dancer for a long time.

Ivan left the building with mixed thoughts and emotions, and as he glanced back at the place that had given him lots of pleasure and satisfaction over the past two years he realized that it was the end of a fantastic part of his life. What the future held for him and his family he didn't dare to think about. His head was buzzing as he started to walk back home. It was only when he'd got a few blocks away that he paused to open his wage envelope, and discovered that he now had almost enough money to last until the end of the year. Petra would be very happy indeed when he got back, thank goodness they lived quite modestly always aware that anything was better than maybe starving in Russia.

Chapter Fourteen

A New Life

The next few weeks went by very quickly for Ivan his sittings with the local artists taking three or four afternoons, and looking after their new son Boris in the mornings whilst Petra was working. The word had got around that he was a good subject to paint owing to his fantastic fitness through dancing. The children thought it was funny that he should be doing such a thing after leading such an active life on stage but what did it matter he was earning a living of sorts. Perhaps it might lead to other things who knows? Some of the quaint artists who dropped into the studios that he worked in puzzled him somewhat. They didn't seem to do much and certainly looked very scruffy, not a bit like the reasonably well off ones that employed him.

It was on one of Ivan's trips to the local market that he was spoken to by a smiling elderly stall holder after purchasing some vegetables.

'You are not at work today M'sieur ?' He said.

Ivan shook his head. 'No not until this evening and sadly my dancing job is finished.'

The man paused a moment. 'Would you like to work a few hours each week for me here then?'

Ivan looked at him a little puzzled. 'You mean selling vegetables? But I've had no experience of doing that.'

'You'll soon learn that M'sier and I've a very good reason for asking you.'

'What's that?' Said Ivan.

The man pointed to the other end of the market.

'You see that other stall with lots of people around it?'

Ivan followed his instructions and saw it was so.

' Well! What of it?'

The stall holder looked serious. 'Well he has employed a man who speaks Russian as well as French and he's getting all the business from the Russian people in Paris. You've got a very nice personality and they all tell me you are quite famous as well in a small way. Go away and think about it and let me know you can work any hours you like as long as they are regular.'

Ivan looked stunned this was an opportunity not to be missed and would fit in nicely with his other jobs. He paused a moment then held out his hand to shake the stallholders.

'Thank you I'll let you know tomorrow what time I'll be free and you let me know the days you want me.'
The man beamed and continued to shake Ivan's hand vigorously.

'I thank you my friend we will do great business together and I look forward to meeting you again tomorrow.'

Ivan smiled and walked away slowly from the market wondering what lay in store for him in this new job, perhaps it might lead to other things and anyway it was the start of something different.

The next day Ivan went back to the market stall and started work. It took him quite some time to learn the prices and how to weigh up the goods, but by the time he left he felt fairly confident about the job. He certainly seemed to attract a lot of Russian speaking customers who wanted to chat with him mainly about life in Paris, the owner of the stall seemed pleased with this sudden increase in business. Ivan left for home a little happier now that he could perhaps earn a bit more over the coming winter.

At his next session at one of the artist's flats he met one called Valentin Serov who seemed anxious to paint him at the first time that he was free. The man had worked on a portrait of Ida Rubenstein and had seen Ivan dance a few times. He spoke about recent life in Russia and seemed very interested in the fact that he'd been the tenant farmer on Prime Minister

Petr Stolypin's estate. He said that Stolypin had been shot and killed at the Kiev Opera House in the presence of the Tzar Nicholas 11 following the passing of some very unpopular laws in Russia. Ivan was shocked at this news especially as Stolypin had treated him personally so well before leaving. Ivan agreed to sit for Serov as soon as one of the artists finished with him, this man certainly seemed most pleasant and very well educated, he'd heard his name mentioned a few times quite recently. It seemed that he'd painted some quite famous portraits in past years Ivan just couldn't understand why this man wanted to paint him of all people.

During the next few weeks he asked some of the artists that he sat for what sort of person Serov was and his standing in the art world, the answer was that he was ranked as one of the worlds best and much sought after. The rich and famous had commissioned him at various times to paint them.

When the time came and Ivan became free to sit for Serov he was aware from the start that the man was not only very talented, but also very knowledgeable about peasant life in Russia and details about the countryside itself. He seemed to take an instant interest in what Ivan told him about life on the farm and folk dancing in particular. His interest in politics amazed Ivan who hadn't had much to do with that side of life apart from the odd meetings with fellow farmers.

After each session with Serov he glanced at the canvas before leaving and knew that this man was so different from most of the others and his work looked somehow more professional and realistic, the sort of detailed pictures that he'd seen hanging in most of the Paris art galleries he'd visited occasionally. This job was to be much shorter than all the others as on the morning of the 22nd of November 1911 Serov suffered a cardiac arrest whilst on his way to a sitting and died immediately at the young age of forty six. Ivan was stunned when he heard the news as he had really got to like this man who had obviously been destined for a brilliant future.

At the funeral shortly afterwards Ivan met many of the cast from the ballet company who had known and worked with Serov over the years. During his lifetime he had painted numerous portraits of famous and titled people and most of the dancers and artistic directors of Russian ballet. He left two unfinished portraits on his death one of Ivan, the other of Princess Polina Shcherbatova whose house he was on his way to visit on the day he died.

Ivan was contacted shortly after Serov's funeral by another artist from Czechoslovakia whose name was Tavik Simon and supposedly quite important in the art world. Ivan did agree to work with him for a short time but didn't like the sort of sketches the man did, he didn't seem to spend much time or effort on them and the likeness was very vague.

As the sittings decreased Ivan spent much more time in the market working and his customers had increased tremendously so much so that the owner gave him a substantial increase in pay. His French was much better now and even the locals used him as he was very humorous when serving them. They found his strange Russian accent so much different from all the other stall people. The children would sometimes pass by with Petra to watch him work and found him most amusing, this was so different a life from his dancing one. He picked up quite a lot of information from some of his customers regarding life in Russia and other news, some of which worried him quite a lot. It seemed that Germany was getting ideas of annexing parts of France and other surrounding countries and the rumours were getting stronger each day. Ivan certainly didn't like the sound of it all and sounded out friends in the market about the possibility of moving on somewhere else. He decided to speak to Petra about it that night knowing that she would probably not want to leave, he knew that she was very happy living in Paris now that things were going well for them.

That evening while Petra was in a reasonably good mood Ivan broached the subject when the children had gone to bed. Sitting in front of the warm fire he plucked up courage and began to question her.

'You really like it here don't you Petra?'

She looked at him and nodded. 'Yes very much, don't you?'

'Of course' he replied. 'But there is talk in the market about a war with Germany and we don't want to get mixed up in that do we?'

'It's only rumour Ivan nothing will come of it you'll see and anyway if we left France where could we go?'

Ivan looked at her for quite some time before answering.

'Well one of my customers has a few small boats leaving for England in the early spring and would be willing to take us there.'

'And how would we pay him for doing this Ivan?'

'Easy really. All he wants is to do a bit of rowing to get there and string a few onions on the way.'

Petra looked at him in amazement. 'But it's a long way to England Ivan supposing the weather is bad?'

Ivan shook his head. 'We will only go on a good day when the forecast is right, and anyway it's not that far really.' Petra didn't look very happy about all this and her face said it all.

'We'll talk about it some other time when and if it all happens, I don't think the Germans will do anything, but we'll see. What will you do for work in England Ivan?'
Ivan was ready for this question as he'd already made inquiries in this direction.

'I have been told that there is a group of artists in London with a Frenchman in it called Lucien Pisarro that will probably use me once we get there, I have got the address where he lives. They call themselves the Camden Town Group and are already quite famous for a certain type of painting. I have already been given a letter of recommendation should we make it to London.'

Ivan felt somewhat relieved that Petra had only half agreed to go without too many objections, but at least they'd talked the problem over together. He decided to watch very carefully over the coming months for signs of war with the German nation and things didn't look too good at all. If there was to be an invasion the Germans wouldn't want Russian refugees living in the heart of Paris. There had been rumours that many Russians were already fleeing to England as a safe place to be, and Ivan loved his family too much to risk their lives in France should war break

Chapter Fifteen

The Crossing

By March 1912 the news came that the Germans had already started making their intentions known about annexing neighbouring lands and troop movements in border towns seemed to bear this out. Ivan by this time had already spoken to an onion boat owner regarding a passage to England for his family on the first available craft. They began to sell off as many bits of furniture as possible to raise the money for their trip from France, they knew that the weather had to be very calm for this to happen so they watched the forecast day by day.

When April came and it started to look more promising they began to pack everything that was light and necessary for the long journey. The children were very exited and every morning thought that they were going that very day, to them every one was the right one. The plan was that once they'd crossed over the water then Petra would go by train with the youngest child Boris to London to find a suitable living place, and await the rest of them who would follow on by other means. They couldn't afford the train fair for all of them as this would not leave enough money for rent during the coming weeks until Ivan found work.

On the day they left Paris by an old horse drawn cart loaded with their scant belongings and knee deep in onions the sun was shining and the future looked good for them at least they hoped so. It was evening the following day when they reached the outskirts of Calais. They searched and found a cheap boarding house to rest in before their epic journey the next day. After unloading their few things necessary for that night they walked down to the harbour with the onion seller to look at the boat that they would be traveling in the next day. It certainly looked big enough for them with two sets of well used strong oars it had probably seen many a similar journey no doubt. The children eyed the boat with amazement they had never seen as large a rowing vessel before, tomorrow was going to be very exiting indeed a day to remember for them all.

The following morning as the family went down the dockside towards the boat with all their prized possessions the sea looked very calm indeed, it was almost good enough to swim across to England. Ivan looked very happy. The weather was better than he'd ever imagined it was certainly going to be their lucky day providing that they made it. Not one of them had ever rowed a boat before and the distance they were about to travel seemed very daunting indeed.

Once aboard with the onion seller in charge they received their instructions from him on what was expected of them during the trip and he then proceeded to push the boat out by means of an oar. The plan was to take it in turns at rowing by the adults with the children plaiting up the onions in bunches as best they could watched over by the seller. Out of the harbour the sea looked a slight bit choppier and the waves a bit more threatening, even so the onion man smiled and said it was a better day than most. So on they went, it was certainly harder work than they had anticipated and both Ivan and Petra soon had sore and blistering hands to show for their efforts.

The children on the other hand seemed to think the whole thing was fun. They'd never seen so many onions in one place before, and were really getting on with the job in a splendid fashion, at the same time the smell of the cargo was very distracting to them.

Having taken it in turns for over an hour at rowing Petra glanced at her hands which were now red and sore she wondered just how much longer she could keep on without having to complain to Ivan. But one look at him nursing his hands convinced her that he was in the same predicament. The onion seller smiled at her and took something from a bag under his seat.

'I've been expecting trouble from your hands Madam so just you wrap this bandage around your fingers with a little cream and you'll be as good as new, then just row a little slower that's all.'

Ivan was watching as Petra took the bandage and cream from him and motioned that he needed the same treatment this journey was going to be far harder than either of them expected.

Three hours into the trip Petra handed round food to them all and they had a brief rest during which the onion seller told them they were almost half way to England. He seemed reasonably confident they would be landing before darkness having made the same journey many times before. Ivan wondered just how he knew they were going the right way as the sea in front looked all the same to him. The children seemed to have lost a bit of their initial enthusiasm and were huddled together under coats asleep in the rear of the boat.

It was only after they had been rowing for just over six hours that Mikael spotted land in the distance and they all followed his finger to confirm the sighting. This gave them a feeling of satisfaction and the thought that the end of the journey was near although in fact it took another hour before they landed a short distance from Dover harbour. With having no passports between them the decision was made that the police or harbour authorities wouldn't take kindly to them. It was there that they took leave of the onion seller and sat with all their bags on the grass near the busy town.

They then went with Petra and Mikael to the railway station to see them off on the long journey to London. All the children were most tearful as well as Petra herself not knowing just how long it would be before she saw them all again. With Ivan and the others waving painfully goodbye the train then slowly left the station Ivan having told Petra to expect them at Victoria Station no sooner than one week later at ten o/clock one morning. They hoped that by the time they all got there she would have found them some suitable cheap lodgings.

Ivan, full of optimism and with only two pounds in English money plus a few francs in his pocket, set off with the rest of the children to walk if necessary the remainder of the way to London. Fortune smiled on them however and a horse drawn farm cart gave them their first lift ten miles beyond the port and better still the farmer let them sleep in his barn for the night, for this they were very grateful as it had been a hard day at sea.

The next morning they all set off after having been given a huge breakfast by the kind farmers wife and good instructions of the way to London. They walked at a leisurely pace for the children's sake so it took quite a few hours to cover the first ten miles, so that by nightfall they started to look for a suitable empty barn or shed to shelter until dawn. The best that they could find was an old disused hay barn with half its roof missing but they managed to shelter there until the first sight of daylight.

Food was getting short by this time so Ivan began collecting wild herbs he knew would be safe from the hedgerows to keep them going. Little did he know how valuable this knowledge would be to one of his children in the years to come, and nettle soup was on the menu most days. They wrote down the names and drew pictures of the plants to give Mikael when they reached him in London. As they got deeper into the English countryside they were offered quite a lot of help by the farmers especially when they discovered that Ivan was himself one of them in his past life. So life on the road for them was proving less difficult than they thought it would be and the children were treating the whole thing as a new fun thing so much better than going to school.

It was day six when they finally reached the outskirts of south London so they knew that one more day should see them at Victoria station and the meeting with their mother at the appointed hour. Petra couldn't believe her eyes as they all trouped into the station looking very weary from their long journey by foot. She somehow felt proud of them, as not many other children could have done the same, and she warmly hugged each of them in turn. Ivan was curious to know what she had found in the way of accommodation for them all if any Petra smiled and nodded in a satisfied way. "Yes we have been very lucky and rented a very small flat not too far from here in a place called the Old Kent Road and it's very nice just above what they call a chip shop." They all looked at her puzzled and Ivan not being familiar with this description of a flat wanted an explanation. 'And what is a chip shop Petra?'

Petra smiled 'It's a place where they fry and sell fish and chipped potatoes that's all.' She replied.

'And is the rent cheap Petra?' Asked Ivan. She nodded. 'Very cheap only three shillings a week and that is because the place smells a bit but it wont bother us too much, and it will do until we find somewhere better.' Young Mikael grinned. 'Wait till we get there you'll see what mother means about the smell it's really different, but you do get used to it after a while and the chips do taste good especially when you are a bit hungry.'

As they approached the new flat in the Old Kent Road the children all looked at one another and pinched their noses as the smell of fish and chips hit them for the first time. Then as Petra led them up the rickety stairs she promised them all their first taste of what was an English delicacy. Later after the meal was over she filled Ivan in on what she'd found out about the owners of the premises and the prospects of getting work in the area. With a look of satisfaction on her face she looked at him and began.

'First of all I have got a part time job in the shop downstairs helping in the evenings My wages more than cover the rent and they are really nice old people. who are going to retire very soon. I have also found a job for you Ivan in the local market that's if you like the people there, that should keep us going for a while perhaps until you find something better. But the best thing of all there is a wonderful ballet company nearby at a place called Covent Garden and with your experience you might just get some work there.'

Ivan looked pleased and surprised that his wife had found out this much in such a short time. 'You have been busy Petra, I really need a few days to recover from our long walk this past week but I'll certainly go and see these market people tomorrow.'

Petra looked at him he certainly looked very weary and slightly older than when she'd last seen him the strain of it all was beginning to show. 'Sorry Ivan. Tell me how hard was the trip?'

Ivan shrugged. 'Quite tiring but we did have a few lucky breaks fortunately and the weather was kind to us with no rain at all.'

What Petra had just told was now gradually beginning to sink in and something was puzzling him.

'Tell me Petra what happens to us if the owners of this place retire and move away?' She smiled. ' I've already found that out it's not for at least another year and after that time they have promised to sell it to us if we want it.'

Ivan looked at her strangely. 'But we have no money and don't know anything about cooking fish and chips.'

Petra seemed taken aback at this response from him. 'Well I've been watching carefully and it all looks very easy to me and I'm sure we will manage to find the money somehow you'll see.'

The next few weeks passed quickly and Ivan managed to secure the job in the market. It was a bit more difficult owing to his almost total lack of English speech. But he slowly got the hang of it to the amusement of most of his customers, some words were very baffling to him but he made a joke of it all and got by. Petra skillfully juggled work in the chip shop and looking after the family with ease and the owners wondered how they had ever managed without her.

The children, once installed in a local school, got on well despite the fact that standards were a little lower than those in their Paris classroom. They were very popular with most of the other pupils owing to the fact that their mother served in the local chip shop and recognized most of them when they came in to be served. As it was one of the few London chip shops where someone spoke and understood the Russian language some of the customers came from long distances to eat there. Just how many other families were living in the city at that time is unknown and Petra knew of hundreds in the same situation as they were.

Ivan managed to eventually get some work at the Opera House but the seasons were few and far between so more of his time was spent in the market than he wanted. Most of the money that he earned there they managed to save in the hope of being able to eventually buy the shop when and if the owners did as they said and retired. One of the consolations he found was that working in the market kept him reasonably fit, he also spent quite a lot of time exploring London on foot and knew almost every part of it within a ten mile radius.

One of his favourite pastimes was listening to the tour guides explaining the historical facts about buildings such as The Tower of London and St Pauls Cathedral. No two of them were alike in their descriptions of the historical facts and Ivan couldn't help smiling at the thought that most of them were probably acting it all out and lead a very boring life at home. On occasional Sundays he took the whole family to the big market at Aldgate to watch the antics of the market traders there selling their wares in the oddest ways. One of which would toss his crockery in the air and managed to catch it without a single breakage, this feat was watched by the biggest crowd of all who stood open mouthed in amazement.

There were drawbacks to moving amongst such large crowds one of which was the amount of pickpockets operating on a regular basis despite the presence of a scattering of police constables, most of whom failed to outrun them when the villains were spotted. In and around the back streets among crowded tenement houses and flats were groups of men playing pitch and toss for halfpennies with one of their number posted to keep an eye open for the local constable.

By this time Ivan, having watched the others frying the fish and chips a few times thought that he ought to have a go just in case they finished up as owners of the shop. The first few tries at this strange way of cooking were a bit hit and miss and one batch was slightly undercooked but afterwards he became quite skilled at the job. The owners told him that they themselves would have employed him in the past had he been around at the time, Ivan though only half believed them but still felt more than a little satisfied with his efforts. Having now lived in the chip shop premises for over a year the owners decided at this point to move on and very kindly sold the business to Ivan and Petra, with just a small down payment and monthly payments to complete the transaction within three years. This pleased the couple immensely who felt that at they were at last really making something of their lives and were hopeful that they might one day save enough to buy or rent a house of some sort.

It was amusing to them both that friends and customers spoke of them as being quite rich, little did they know how much they owed for supplies and rent, but they both still felt confident of being able to make a good living somehow. Although the work was hard it was easier than their life had been in Russia and it was made even better now that Sundays were theirs to all go out together and enjoy themselves. Little did they know how events were about to change their lives forever in just a few short months.

Chapter Sixteen

War

It was quite a shock in late 1914 when a strange looking letter arrived one morning for Ivan it looked very important and he turned a strange colour when he read the contents of it. Petra watched him for a few moments before asking as to what it was.

'What is it Ivan?'

Ivan put the letter down grim faced. 'It says I've been called up for the army my love and to report next week.'

Petra looked at him puzzled. 'But they said only last week they had enough young volunteers so why you of all people?'

Ivan nodded. 'That's what everyone says. Perhaps they are short now that the war looks more certain' He glanced at the letter again then handed it to Petra who studied it anxiously.

'That's terrible Ivan! However will we manage without you?'

'I don't know but you will I'm sure my love, you must be brave. This war won't last long half the world is against the Germans this time including Russia.'

Petra put the letter down on the table and hugged him with tears in her eyes. 'How are we going to explain this all to the children?'

'Leave it to me Petra I'll explain it all to them later today and they will all help you in the shop when they can, if you need some extra help just get some on the busy days. It won't cost too much and there's plenty of ladies around here need the money especially those whose husbands are away in the war.'

Later that day Ivan took the children aside and explained just what had happened and after a few tears they all promised to look after their mother whilst Ivan was away. This would be the first time they'd been apart since leaving France and the thought of it really disturbed them although the two oldest ones tried not to show it too much.

The following week came much too soon for the whole family and lots of tears were shed as Ivan left them at the station on his way to the barracks, carrying as much personal clothing as he was allowed. Petra wondered just how long it would be before she would see him again and said a quiet prayer for his safe return. All around them were hundreds of much younger men all laughing and joking as though they were off on holiday without a care in the world. Petra wondered if they fully realized just what they were getting into and how many of them would be coming back alive after the war finished. As the train slowly steamed out of the station they all waved goodbye to Ivan who leaned out of the carriage window sad faced.

As they walked slowly back home Petra had difficulty answering awkward questions from the children as to why their father should have to leave them so suddenly. She felt like crying her eyes out at this moment but held herself in check for fear of making the situation worse, and it would be many weeks before she could come to terms with what had happened.

It was in August that Britain officially declared war on Germany and Petra had by this time received a letter from Ivan who said he was alright and expecting to be posted somewhere abroad very soon, but couldn't say where as they were told not to speak about it.

By the middle of September came the news of a big battle in Aisne Belgium and it was rumoured that thousands of troops were killed and wounded. Petra prayed every night that nothing had happened to Ivan and that he might still be in England after all. Another letter from Ivan came dated early September from somewhere in England full of how he missed her and the children and hopes of getting leave soon. But sadly it was not to be as she was informed shortly after this that he was missing presumed dead in Belgium. This was followed months later by a letter confirming his death and awarding her a small pension which seemed to her a miserable amount for the loss of a man's life. She was now left with four children to keep and a shop to run on her own in a strange country and very few real friends.

It took quite some time to recover from the shock and decide how to break the news to the children that their father was never coming home again. Just how many other families were in the same predicament soon became clear as customers coming into the shop told the same sad story, and most were in a worse financial situation than her. Being the kind person that she was Petra let some of the more genuine ones off paying at times to help them over this bad period of their lives. Each night she cried herself to sleep wondering if she'd ever come to terms with having lost the love of her life like this, it was only the thought of having to care for the children that kept her going now. A month after she started receiving her widow's pension Petra was startled to find a battered envelope inside her front door and with shaking hands opened it slowly, the writing was unmistakable, it from Ivan.

My Dearest Petra. You cannot imagine what it is like here where we are there are so many bodies lying around that the medics are not able to cope with them all. The local people are burying as many nearby as they can. I hope and pray that it will all soon be over and we can all come home again. All my love to you all.

Ivan.

It was obvious from the state of the envelope itself that it had barely survived at all with spots of blood and mud on it. Petra wept as she read it many times before putting it safely with the others from him, it was one of the worst moments of her life. How on earth was she going to survive the rest of the war

By early 1917 Petra had at last paid off the rest of the money to the previous owners of the shop and it was now hers. Now she could think about maybe renting a small more modern flat somewhere close to live in and rent out their existing smelly flat. It took quite a few weeks to locate somewhere reasonably close by at Herne Hill, a place with a small but tidy garden for the children to play in and they were thrilled with it. They had to change schools which involved buying the uniforms for them all but they soon settled in and were doing well at their lessons. It was hard to get used to the journey to and from the shop each day but the difference in the new house made up for it in the end. Petra felt sure that within just a few short years she would be able to sell the business and get a part time job somewhere in Herne Hill.

This had been a year of bad news from Russia where a revolution had taken place and the slaughter of the Tsar Nicholas and his whole family shook the world. Little did Petra realize how close England came to it's own revolution the next year when the troops came home to mass unemployment, and those that did find work earned very little money. In the face of mass strikes and civil disturbances the government finally backed down and the unions forced up wages all round.

During the following years the progress of the children was quite amazing considering they had arrived not knowing much of the language. The youngest, Boris, had the best start and really picked up on it from scratch and by the time he went to school was very fluent and bright with it. Nika on reaching thirteen started working in a dress shop nearby and helped Petra keep the house tidy in her spare time. Anna, the oldest of them, was now in service at the home of a very rich family in the west-end and just came home on odd weekends when she could.

Although Petra had by now got used to living without Ivan the memory of their life together still stayed fresh in her mind and just small things like walking down the street seeing other couples hand in hand really was painful to her. She wondered if she'd ever come to terms with it and no other man could ever take Ivan's place at this point in her life. Now that the war was over things were getting a little better with food just a little more plentiful despite being rationed still she managed to keep them all reasonably well fed and clothed.

So with one girl working and living away and another one earning her keep things were much better financially for Petra. Her neighbours were an odd lot and mostly middle class who kept themselves aloof from her family because they thought her definitely working class and just not up to their standard at all. Petra wasn't too bothered anyway, what they thought about her as she had her own close friends who could be relied on in case of problems.

When Christmas came in 1917 they had a grand party with all the children and friends invited which they celebrated in real Russian style to the amazement of all their London friends. Later that evening some of young children's friends began to ask Petra questions about the family's flight from Russia and she began to wonder just what the older children had already told them. She began with just a few basic facts that even Mickael and Boris knew nothing about after which one asked just how good a dancer was her late husband.

'Well a very good one really although only ever to support the likes of Vaslav Nijinski on stage who at that time was rated as the best dancer in the world.' She replied. The children all looked very impressed at this statement. Then one young boy named Robert asked how dangerous it had been on the journey through Europe. Petra smiled. 'Not really! Just a few wild animals and some of the mountains that we had to cross on the way.'

The children seemed well satisfied with Petra's answers and probably couldn't wait to gather further information at a later date, they had all had an exiting day and couldn't wait to tell their parents all about it.

When Mikael reached his thirteenth birthday he was picked to go to an art college having achieved the highest marks in the exams at school that year. He was told that his work was some of the best that had ever been produced by someone so young. So good were his marks that he gained a place at the Camberwell College of Art that year, this was indeed good news because it was so near home for him. This was to prove the turning point in his future life and he took care to learn as much as possible backed up with visits to all the well known London galleries and museums at every opportunity. He was questioned by Petra about the college one evening shortly after joining and she was puzzled by some of his answers so she delved deeper feeling that he was holding something back.

'What do you really think about your new school Mikael?' She asked.

He thought about it for a few moments before replying.

'Well it's quite good but....' Petra felt he wasn't going to tell her just what it was that he found wrong so she tried to look a little stern for once.

'But what! That isn't a very good answer is it?' She said.

Mikael looked away uneasily wondering how his mother would react to what he had to tell her.

'Well it's not really what I expected it to be like. Some of the other boys seem to treat it all like a joke they think art is sticking bits of wood and paper together and the teachers are letting them get away with it.' Petra smiled with relief that if that was all his problem was then she had all the answers for him.

'Funny you should say that many years ago your father said the very same thing about some of the very famous artists that he sat for, he thought they were a bit crazy at the time. But now those very same pictures are worth fortunes. There's no accounting for some peoples taste, it takes all sorts to make up this world Mikael so don't worry about it just paint the way you want.'

Mikael looked happier at this answer and felt pleased that his mother understood what he meant, he hadn't really expected her to at all. What he hadn't told her was that quite a lot of the students were acting very funny at times and that he'd caught some of the boys embracing in the toilet areas more than once, he was at this moment too embarrassed to speak about that to her. He was altogether a very sensitive and shy boy and spent a lot of time thinking about how the pupils around him were behaving. There were quite a mix of boys at the school but mainly from the surrounding area and a lot whose fathers had been killed in the war like his, some of these he befriended almost at once. Those he didn't like were from the middle class homes further away who seemed to think they were the superior ones. Mikael steered well clear of these, he thought they were not to be trusted at all unlike the boys he'd got used to around the Old Kent Road despite the scrapes they sometimes got into.

Chapter Seventeen

Anna

Walking through the crowded shopping streets in the centre of London on one of her rare mid weekdays off Anna reflected on the strange life that she lived now that she was 19 years old. This was totally different from the fairly strict family upbringing she had been used to and she wondered just what her father would have thought about it all. She had moved up the ladder in the house of the Bolton family and was now an upstairs maid and was responsible for looking after Mrs Bolton's bedroom, wardrobe, and personal grooming unlike the job of daily cleaning and washing up as a kitchen maid when first she started there.

She was now a permanent staff member unlike some who seemed to last only a few weeks before they were dismissed as unsuitable. Mrs Bolton was so pleased with her work that she gave her the occasional clothes to keep, mainly to show her off in when important visitors came to dine at the house. Her boss was always telling her friends that really good servants such as Anne should not be seen in uniform at family functions and that they should be made to feel part of the family. Just what her friends really thought about such matters goodness only knows, thought Anna, every other servant she spoke to thought Mrs Bolton quite extremely mad.Poor Mr Bolton, a very timid sort of person usually just sat thereand said nothing most of the time as his wife was never lost for words, he just nodded in agreement with her at table.

Anna managed to give her mother a few shillings every trip home to help her out financially as there were still young Boris and Mickael to clothe and feed, her sister Nika was now earning enough to help mother with the rent. Each time she went home her mother looked a little older and the lines in her face were a bit more visible Anna knew this was down to the years of really hard work and the worry of bringing them all up. The comparison with Mrs Bolton was quite different she had probably never done a day's work in her life and it really showed. The woman was about the same age as Petra but looked ten years younger. Anna knew that somehow she would try and get on in life by visiting the local library and learning as much as possible in order to get perhaps a better job. It seemed that the girls who worked in offices earned quite a lot more than she did, and the long hours she worked prevented her from going to night classes to get some sort of qualifications. In one of the shops she sometimes visited the owner being a Frenchman spoke to her in French and said her prospects would be good in a firm with foreign connections. Anna was too modest to tell him she also spoke a little Italian and fluent Russian as well this would really amaze him.

With these thoughts on her mind Anna spotted an advert in a shop window for a French speaking secretary so on the spur of the moment she wrote it down and walked slowly on to the nearby square. Once there she sat on a bench and studied the details of the advert, then having noticed the place was within walking distance she made up her mind to chance her luck and check it out. It only took a few minutes to reach the office in nearby Soho where she studied the outside of the building. To her it looked a respectable establishment so she quickly went inside and approached the lady on the reception desk.

With the note in her hand she tried to remain calm and decisive.

'I've called about your advertisement for a French speaking secretary.'

The lady looked her up and down before replying.

'And have you got an appointment Miss?'

Anna was surprised at this answer. 'No, not really do I need to?'

'Yes usually but what is your French like?'

Anna paused. 'Very good! That is I think so.'

The woman picked up the telephone slowly still looking at Anna and cranked the handle of the small switchboard then when a voice answered she spoke softly into the telephone.

'There's a lady here sir about the vacancy says her French is very good, shall I send her in to you?'

The receptionist then replaced the phone and smiled at Anna. 'Mr Graham will see you now follow me and I'll show you his room.' Anna walked slowly up two flights of stairs where the receptionist pushed open the door marked Manager and motioned Anna to enter.

As she walked towards Mr Graham's desk he politely stood up and held out his hand to welcome her. As she shook his hand he motioned her to sit down in a nearby seat.

'Good morning Miss! So you've come about the job then?

Anna nodded nervously. 'Yes I saw your advertisement in a shop window earlier today.'

Mr Graham picked up a pencil and eyed the very neat and very good looking young girl seated in front of him hoping that she would meet all his requirements.

'First of all I need to know your name miss?' He said.

'Anna Garodny Sir' she replied.

'And your age please?'

'Nineteen.'

'And where are you working at present then? ' He asked.

Anna thought for a few seconds before replying.

'Well Sir I'm in service at the moment but my employer relies on me a lot to answer her letters especially those written in French.'
So far so good thought Mr Graham now comes the tricky part.

'What experience have you with a typewriter then?'

'Yes of course I have and my mother lets me use hers at home, and I'm reasonably fast on it.' said Anna.

Mr Graham smiled at this answer, this young girl just didn't seem right for the position but having started to interview her he had to carry on and give her the benefit of the doubt.

'I understand your French is good then?'

'Yes we lived there for quite a while when I was younger and I also speak and can write in Russian.' Anna replied.

At this Mr Graham looked very surprised he'd never yet met any person so young with knowledge of the Russian language, this was very unusual indeed. Perhaps she might be useful after all. He sometimes dealt with Russian fur companies and had to have their letters translated, and that always took time to do. He started to write down a few notes. This interview was getting a few unexpected results, this girl was not the usual sort he'd seen in the past and she spoke quite nicely as well.

'How is it you speak Russian then?'

Anna looked a little pleased with herself at this question.

'That's where I was born and my mother still speaks the language most of the time at home.'

The manager was reasonably satisfied with Anna's answer but decided to test her a little on this point and took a letter from his desk drawer and passed it to Anna to look at. She took it and looked at him quizzically.

'Can you tell me what it says in English please Anna?'

Very slowly Anna began to read aloud the contents of the short Russian letter.

'Dear Sir. Please forward as soon as possible payment for the small parcel of furs we sent you recently hoping that they were to your satisfaction.'

Mr Graham smiled at this moment, this was the girl he was looking for, someone who could be of help in the office and also looked presentable when rich clients called on him. He held out his hand to retrieve the letter then put it back on the desk.

'When could you start work for us then Anna?'

'You mean I've got the job then?'

'Of course! The manager replied, 'How much notice do you have to give your present employer?'

Anna just couldn't believe her luck and her face showed it.

'Probably a month sir but I might get away sooner without upsetting Mrs Bolton maybe, and also I will have to find somewhere cheap to live unless I go back home again.'

Mr Graham looked thoughtful for a moment. 'Maybe it might help if you moved in upstairs. We have an empty flat on the top floor, it's a bit small but you could have it very cheaply. Perhaps you'd like to have a look at it?'

Anna's mind was in a whirl at this offer perhaps there was more to this than she thought what if this man was after more than a secretary. She'd read about such goings on in this part of London. But for now she'd better play along with him and look at the flat so as not to insult him by turning his offer down. Perhaps it would be cheaper to take his offer than to pay the fares from her mothers house at Herne Hill each day, and it would give her the chance to explore the area and maybe improve her educational skills in the evenings. She smiled at the manager and stood up ready to accept his tour of the flat.

'I'd love to have a look at the flat please.' She said.

Having waited what seemed to him like ages for an answer the Manager then stood up and took the keys from a hook on the wall and moved to the door followed by the curious Anna.

On reaching the upstairs flat Anna was more than surprised at the size of it and the general cleanliness she found there, she smiled and decided at once to accept the offer of tenancy of it providing the rent was reasonable.

'How much is the rent for this flat?' Asked Anna. The manager smiled.

'Well providing your work is satisfactory you can have it free the only cost will be the electricity.'

This was really a surprise to Anna one that she didn't expect it was going to be the start of a new life for her and she couldn't wait to tell her mother of her good luck and the extra freedom that it would bring her. She looked carefully at all the rooms the flat contained and although she was more than a little surprised that the job had come her way so much more easily than she had expected, it was however hers now and she vowed to make something of it.

On her way out she thanked the manager most profusely for his offer of the job, and promised to let him know quickly the exact date that she would be able to start work for him.

Chapter Eighteen

The Letter

When Anna went home a few days later and it was with a satisfied smile on her face that she told her mother of her new job in an office. Petra was taken by surprise at this news it was indeed something she had not anticipated as Anna had always seemed happy with her job in service, She let her talk about her new job for quite some time before speaking.

'But Anna are you quite sure about this change in your work? This does seem too good to be true and the free rent of the flat should be more than a bit suspicious, I do hope that you're right in taking it.'
Anna smiled and nodded. 'Of course I am mother, besides the manager had such an honest face and it's mainly because I speak Russian that he's given me the job.'

Petra still wasn't totally convinced that the job was a genuine one.

'Well I hope you are right but it just seems a bit too good to be true lets hope that it turns out alright for your sake.'
Petra moved towards a nearby cupboard and took out a letter which she then opened.

'I've had letter from our relations in France and they are all well and send their love. The war was not too good for them but they managed to survive it reasonably well. The children are all grown up and working now and have good honest jobs, that is except for the eldest girl Galina, she unfortunately is selling her body to men in a fashionable part of Paris. Her parents are disgusted and don't want anything more to do with her now.'

Anna thought carefully for a few seconds before replying.

'Perhaps she couldn't get any other sort of job that pays enough to live on mother and anyway it's her life and that's what she's chosen to do, who are we to judge her and Paris I've been told is a very expensive place to live in after all.'

'That is why I want you to be careful Anna with this person who wants to give you a flat rent free it seems very suspicious to me, are you sure he is a genuine employer?'

Anna frowned at this question from her mother and although not absolutely certain of the man's total honesty, thought it best to at least say something to convince her that she knew the job was alright.

'Just leave it to me mother nothing will happen I am quite old enough to take care of myself.'

Petra decided that perhaps she'd better let the matter drop and change the subject.

'The letter says that they all live on a farm just outside Paris and actually own it having worked there until the owner died and left it to them in his will.'

Anna's face brightened. 'Are they rich now then mother?'

'No not really. Its only a small farm with just a few cattle and a small vineyard just big enough to give them a reasonable living, perhaps one day we'll save up enough to go and see them.'

Petra although quite pleased to receive the letter from her relatives in France was sad to think that they didn't know that Ivan had died in the war, and that she'd have to tell them this in her reply.

'When I write to them Anna I will mention that we might come and see them all one day and perhaps stay a few days, that would be nice wouldn't it?'

'That would be something to look forward to mother we haven't seen them for years now the children must be grown up and really like proper French people.'

Petra nodded. 'Let's hope that we can save a little and really try and go there soon Anna.' As she finished speaking there was a knock on the door,

Petra hurried to answer it and a tall well dressed man stood there smiling.

'Good afternoon! Are you Mrs Garodny?

Petra nodded wondering who could this stranger be.

'Yes that's me. What do you want?'

'My name is Roberts and I'm from your son Mikael's school, may I come in and have a chat, there is some good news for you I hope.'

Petra looked puzzled at this statement but beckoned the man in and led him into the front room. Once seated Mr Roberts took out a letter from his coat pocket and glanced at it.

'It seems that one of the schools patrons has taken a liking to your son's work as an artist and wants him to go to Paris to further his studies. This gentleman has connections with the Leonardo da Vinci School there and is willing to pay all his fees and expenses for three years, that is of course if you agree to it. The man in question is of course above reproach and very rich he is also on the board at The National Gallery and has seen the potential in your sons work.'

Petra seemed surprised at this man's news and it took quite a few moments before she answered. 'This is wonderful if it's true but Mikael is only fourteen years old isn't he a bit young to do this?'

Mr Roberts shook his head smiling. 'No, not really, this is the time when extra tuition really pays dividends and he obviously has the talent to take him almost to the top of the art world in a very short time. And what is not generally known is that the great Leonardo da Vinci himself was only fourteen years old when he started tuition as a painter.'

Petra looked very surprised. 'What exactly has he done to deserve this attention?'

'It was his ability to not only copy famous works of art but the detail of his copied work would defy even experts, and the subjects are mainly religious works and difficult ones at that.' Replied Mr Roberts.

Petra sat there not knowing what to say next and although she knew that Mikael was very intelligent and his art work above average she didn't realise he was quite that good. At times she had been shown the odd drawing by him and praised him for it but this offer was certainly unexpected.

'If I agree to let him go when will this take place?' She said.

'When the new term begins in Paris three weeks from now so we would like your approval fairly quickly so as to make arrangements for his enrolment there.'

Petra wondered what Ivan would have thought about this had he been still alive to witness this event, he would have been so proud of his son no doubt. Now that she'd recovered from the initial shock she decided to agree to let the boy go that is if he wanted to and he'd be silly to pass this chance up.

She stood up smiling and held her hand out to agree with the offer and Mr Roberts grasped it warmly.

'Thank you sir I will talk to my son tonight and I'm sure that he will want to go to Paris, although his French is a little rusty after being in England so long but I'm sure he will manage alright.'

Mr Roberts satisfied that his journey had been worthwhile then made to leave.

'I hope Mrs Garodny that you are as proud of your son as we all are at the college and that we get equally good reports from Paris when he starts there.'

Petra smiled with satisfaction before showing her visitor out and couldn't wait to tell Anna in the other room the good news.

As she closed the front door and turned around a curious Anna was waiting anxiously to hear what it was all about.

'Who was that man mother? What did he want?'

Petra walked towards the kitchen with Anna following.

'He was from Mikael's school Anna and they want him to go to Paris to a famous art school there.'

On reaching the kitchen Anna with a puzzled look on her face sat on a stool and faced her smiling mother.

'How will he get there then?'

'Somehow I will have to take him. That's if I can afford the fare of course.'

'But you haven't any spare money mother have you?'

'No but I'll find it somehow you'll see, and it will be a chance to visit our relations near Paris whilst I'm there.'

'And what about the shop mother who will you get to run it while you're gone?'

'Don't worry Anna the couple who help me now are quite capable of managing it and they will be grateful for some extra money, besides they have been asking me for ages to sell them the business now perhaps is the right time to do it.'

Anna frowned at this statement this was something she hadn't even thought about. This might upset her plans for the new job.

'But mother what about Boris and Nika who will look after them while you are gone?'

'That is something I have to think about Anna, as a last resort I'll have to take Boris with me, and Nika is quite old enough to take care of herself for a few weeks.'

Later that day when Mikael returned from school Anna asked him if he knew the full extent of the award he had been given and if he was pleased and wanted to accept it. Smiling he sat down after placing his school satchel on the nearby table.

'Of course I want to go mother this is terrific news and very unexpected as the headmaster only told me the brief details this afternoon.' Petra thought he seemed more than grateful that someone he didn't know would think him good enough to spend a large amount on his further education and couldn't believe his luck. He then went on to show his mother some of the best samples of his school work that gained him the top marks of the previous term. The pictures that she saw were absolutely stunning, the like of which she had only seen before in the best galleries in Paris many years ago.

She sat there hardly believing her eyes at the quality of his work, no wonder somebody wanted to help him with his fees in Paris, but just who could it be? She knew that she was very soon to find out just who that person was after her trip, to Paris. But the task she now faced was how to raise enough money to take Mikael to his new college in Paris and also to sell the fish and chip shop quickly.

After supper Petra took all the children into the living room to explain what had happened earlier in the day knowing that they would have talked together about her intended trip to Paris.

'So now that you've all had a good chat together, about the man who called on me today, I'd better tell you what might happen in a few weeks time.'

'If I can get the money to go to Paris and that's not certain yet I may then decide to take Boris as well as Mikael so that will only leave you Nika, to look after the house while we are away.'

This statement didn't seem to please Nika and her face showed it.

'Why can't I come as well mother?' she said.

Petra shook her head. 'It will be expensive enough with three of us going and it may take longer than a week to find Mikael somewhere to live and be sure he's alright there, and anyway what about your job? Your employers wouldn't like you being away that long would they?'

'I don't like my job very much mother.' Replied Nika. 'And I was thinking of leaving anyway but you seem to have made up your mind already so I'll just have to stay I suppose, perhaps I'll look around for another job while you're gone.'

'Good! Replied Petra. 'That might keep you busy then and as a reward we'll promise to bring you back a nice present from Paris for looking after the house Nika.'

This seemed to satisfy Nika but she still didn't relish the thought of living alone in the house without the others.

Anna who had been sitting quietly in the corner thought she'd cheer her sister up a little with a suggestion.

'Well Nika I have to work my notice out for a few weeks yet so at least I promise to come round on my day off to see you, also you can always telephone me at work if anything bothers you.'

'Thank you Anna that's nice of you. Said Petra smiling. 'Now I think it's time for bed there's nothing more we can do until I can raise the money anyway, we'll let you know Anna next week how things are, it might all happen sooner than we think.'

Chapter Nineteen

Return to Paris

The next two weeks were hectic ones for Petra but she managed somehow to get an agreement from the people in the shop and a good down payment for it, with proper legal papers to confirm the rest of the following installments. She now had more than enough money to take Mikael to Paris and stay long enough to visit the rest of the family providing of course she could find them. Her biggest problem was trying to arrange her trip across the channel as only military personnel and government officials were allowed on the available boats. Although there was no fighting going on anywhere near Paris further east it was still a danger zone.

One of the officers in Ivan's regiment was more than helpful and got Petra authorization for their passage but only just in time for the start of the school term. He did warn her that it might just be an uncomfortable journey for them as passenger boats were in short supply.When the day arrived that Petra, Mikael, and Boris said a tearful farewell to the other two children at Victoria Station the whole place was packed with servicemen,who were going back to France, returning to battle after leave or nervous new recruits. Petra managed to get a seat for them all near the front of the train and the two older children spent almost the whole journey with their heads out of the carriage window apart from the odd tunnels.

On arrival at Dover they followed the crowd to the dockside and checked for the boat they were booked on. It turned out to be a very basic transport vessel with very few facilities or toilets. They spent the whole crossing on deck alongside mainly soldiers laughing and joking as though they were going on holiday, it was certainly a weird experience.

After a long drawn out train journey to Paris with lots of stops on the way due to signal failures on the line they finally got to the capital three hours late tired and exhausted. Petra had already planned to start her search for accommodation in the district that they had lived in previously near the market and was astonished on arrival there to find the whole place buzzing with activity.

Not wanting to disturb her friends too early they had coffee in a nearby cafe before calling on them for information about a cheap flat. So pleased were one family to see them back that they offered to put them up temporarily for the cost of their food during their stay. Petra was pleased with this kind offer and decided to visit the market for some food in response to this gesture. On her arrival inside the market she was amazed at the buzz of the place it was as though the war never existed there seemed to be plenty of everything unlike in England where food was very short indeed.

The next two hectic days were spent sorting themselves out before taking Mikael to his new college which was fortunately only a short walking distance away on the Avenue de Villars set in very stunning grounds. As they waited in the reception area to meet the head teacher Mikael sat staring in wonderment at at the ornate furniture and decoration of the place. The whole ceiling was filled with murals similar to the ones he'd done at his last school and he just couldn't take his eyes off them.

As the head teacher entered the room both mother and son were struck by his appearance he wasn't dressed like the teachers back in London and looked so smart. After greeting them both he picked up a file from his desk and smiled.

'It is with great pleasure that I welcome you to one of the most famous and important art colleges in the world, you Mikael have been recommended by somebody very important as an outstanding pupil. Many of the world's most talented artists have passed through these doors and have gone on to fame and fortune. I sincerely hope that the same will happen to you Mikael and with a few years guidance from us you will do the same.' They both sat there astonished at the mans complimentary remarks and Petra thought what a shame that Ivan hadn't lived long enough too see this all happening to his son. Mikael also felt slightly embarrassed that anyone should speak so well of him at this stage in his life he was after all still very young. He was also aware that this particular place was named after one of the most famous artists of all time Leonardo da Vinci. Also on the wall opposite him was a huge list of all the most famous artists who'd passed through the college over the years.

Petra had decided to come one day earlier than she had been told just in case there was a problem with the accommodation but there turned out to be none, and they gave him the key to a very small but neat room which he would be sharing with another boy. The following day they took Mikael back to enroll and start his term. They wished him luck, kissed him goodbye and promised to return and visit him after trying to find their relations at the farm on the outskirts of Paris.

Chapter Twenty

The Farm

Petra thought that she knew roughly where their relations lived just outside Paris but it took her and Boris quite some time to find the village where the farm was located. On finally reaching it Petra was surprised at the look of the place it was very run down and not at all what she'd expected. The whole place looked neglected with the gate off its hinges and paint peeling off all the woodwork on the house, even the scraggy dog that barked at them looked half starved.

Ivan's brother Yuri had the door open with a big smile on his face and greeted them both with warm hugs and kisses, he looked years older than when they'd last met.

'Come on in I'll go and fetch Olga she's in the barn.'

He showed them into the front room and left to find his wife Olga and while he was gone Petra studied the room carefully it looked slightly better than the outside suggested. Although the furniture was old it was solid and good quality with a shine on it the result of many hours of polishing. There was a lovely smell about the place part wax polish and also cooking which made Petra feel a little hungry.

On his return Yuri had a smiling Olga with him so there was more hugs and kisses after which she stood back and studied them both shaking her head.

'My you both look so well.' She cried. And how are the other three children?'

'They're fine Olga. 'We've just left Mikael at his new college in Paris, Anna has just started a new job in an office in London and Nika works in a dress shop not far from our house. But how are all your young ones?' Olga took a deep breath before replying. 'Well you already know all about our Galina and her nasty business in Paris I'll give you her address if you like and it's up to you if you want to visit her, but telephone first, she might be busy with a client as she calls them. Natalya is a good girl and works in a shop in the next village so we just know she won't come to any harm there, and Dimitri has his own lorry and is delivering wine at the moment and should be home soon.'

At this point Yuri intervened to make a suggestion. 'Would you like to stay with us Petra a few days we have plenty of room here?'
Petra seemed pleased at this invitation. 'Thank you Yuri that's kind of you we'd love to but only for one night if that's alright with you both.'

'Sure stay longer if you want to.' Replied Petra.

'Thank you but one night would be lovely. We promised to visit Mikael once before going back to England.'

The visit went well and they learnt all about how to live and run a farm in France under wartime conditions. The family seemed to live reasonably well despite having to conceal Yuri and Dimitri at odd times from the Germans. They were helped quite often by the very active French resistance forces who tipped them off when the Germans came near the farm. One of the most frightening times of the war was the shelling early that year of Paris by the Germans with their new super gun the like of which had never been seen before. Even being quite a few miles out from the capital they still heard the sound of it and the news of how many civilians daily it was killing.

Leaving was painful for them all but Petra promised to return should she come to visit Mikael at college the following year, she had made up her mind at this point to visit Galina as well in Paris before leaving just out of curiosity. Perhaps the girl wasn't as bad as her mother made out she seemed a nice girl all those years ago.

The next day she went with Boris to try and see Galina in the centre of Paris and was greeted with hugs and kisses ,she just knew it had to be a very tactful visit one where she had to choose her words very carefully.

'I had a letter from your mother recently' Said Petra.' 'And she said you were doing very nicely on your own but didn't like the way you were earning your living especially as you were brought up as a catholic.'

Galina smiled at this remark. 'My mother is a bit old fashioned. This was my decision and it's a good a way as any other of making a living and the rewards are that I can retire in a few short years if I'm careful. I pick my clients from the very rich ones in Paris and I already own this nice flat here. My parents are still struggling to earn a living on that farm they'll never own but I've got enough money to help them if they really need it.' Petra thought this was something very kind and maybe the girl was a much better person than her mother gave her credit for and she aught to accept the situation as it was. Next time she wrote to her mother she'd mention it tactfully. She looked around the flat noticing just how neat and tidy it was and furnished very expensively much better than anything she herself could afford. As she left she kissed Galina goodby and promised to write to her when she returned to London.

After seeing Mikael settled into school and a small shared flat nearby Petra left for London with Boris happy that everything had gone so well for him, even though he'd said he would miss them all a lot Paris seemed a much better place to live in despite the war still going on in eastern France and everyone seemed so friendly. This had been a good part of her past life, if only Ivan could have lived a little longer to see his children grow up how happy he'd have been.

Chapter Twenty One

A Seat on the Board

Arriving back home Petra was faced with a mountain of letters one of which looked quite important she recognised the envelope as being from The Camberwell School of Art. On opening it she studied the contents for quite some time before she understood what they wanted it was more than a surprise for her. It seemed that they wanted her in view of her sons achievement to sit on the board of Governors at the college something that didn't seem possible to her from such a humble background. The letter had been written a few days earlier whilst they had been in France so they probably wanted a reasonably early reply, so she telephoned the secretary later that afternoon. She asked why she of all people had been chosen and the answer was that she was the mother of their most outstanding pupil for years.

After taking a few seconds to take in all that she was told Petra said that she'd attend the next meeting the following week and hoped to be suitable for the board. It was only after putting the phone down that the full implication of what she'd done hit her, surely there must be a more qualified parent could do it better than her. Something was a bit fishy about it all maybe all would be revealed next week.

It took quite a few days to get back to normal life after the Paris trip and through it all Petra couldn't help thinking about her forthcoming meeting at the school, and every day she worried a little more. Nothing in her past life had prepared her for such a strange task this was indeed a trip into the unknown. She wondered if her Russian accent would let her down speaking to all those posh people at the college, and what if they found out she'd been the owner of a common fish and chip shop? It didn't bear thinking about in for a penny in for a pound as her old customers would have said.

When the day of the meeting arrived Petra dressed in what she thought suitable presented herself at the Art College a few minutes earlier than the appointed time and was escorted into a large study with walls filled with the most attractive paintings she'd ever seen in a school. Already present was a smartly dressed middle aged man and a very attractive younger woman the man smiled and walked towards Petra with hand extended.

'You must be Petra Garodny ?' He said shaking her hand warmly.

'Yes that's right I seem to be a bit early.' The man shook his head.

'No you are here in good time let me introduce myself I am Charles Philips chairman of the meeting and this is Jane Thomas our secretary.' Petra moved forward and nervously shook Jane's hand. Charles motioned to Petra to take a seat close to the top of the table.

'I will of course introduce you properly to the rest when they all arrive which will be quite soon.' He said. 'And if you just listen to what is discussed here you will soon get the hang of it, it's all quite simple and straight forward.'

By the end of the meeting Petra was feeling a lot less nervous and Charles asked her to stay behind to discuss something with her. It was only when the others had left that he spoke quietly to her. 'I hope that you didn't find us too boring Petra we do ramble on a bit over what seems trivial things?'

She shook her head. 'No not at all it was very interesting.'

'That's good! Now perhaps I can make a little confession. You probably wondered how you came to be asked to join this group?' Petra smiled hesitantly. 'Yes of course I did.'

'Well it was mainly because of your son's achievements as a most promising pupil and we were all thrilled when he got the place in Paris. We all went out to celebrate when we heard the news. So Petra it would please me immensely if you would have dinner with me sometime soon?' Petra looked at him wondering what all this was about as nobody had asked her out in the past she waited a few moments before answering.

'Can I let you know Charles, I'll have to make arrangements first?'

'Certainly here's my telephone number call me when it's

convenient.'Petra took his card said goodbye and left the building wondering whether to accept this total stranger's offer, this was indeed something new to her

The following week Petra called Charles to say that she could see him a few days later and was stunned when he said their meeting would be at the Savoy Hotel in the west end, what on earth should she wear for such an occasion? After careful thought and a quick bit of dressmaking and alteration she soon found a few suitable garments that would pass scrutiny in such a posh place. She now felt confident that her clothes would pass scrutiny and that she wouldn't look out off place there

When she arrived at the Savoy on the appointed evening Charles was already there waiting seated by the reception desk he got up to greet her smiling, she certainly was an attractive lady with the most fantastic hair of any woman he'd ever met, she was absolutely stunning.

'Good evening Petra! I'm so glad you made it I think our table is almost ready but would you like a drink first in the lounge?'
Petra nodded. 'Thank you! That would be nice Charles.'

It was only later when they'd almost finished eating that Charles decided to ask Petra about herself.

'You probably don't know this but I was one of the people that interviewed your son about his place in the Paris college, and some very interesting facts were brought to our attention about yourself and the family.'

'Really! And what did Mikael say then?'Replied Petra.

'Oh mainly about your journey across Europe from Russia it was most interesting to us as we'd never come into contact with anyone who'd done such a fantastic thing.'

Petra smiled at this. "It wasn't all that unusual really thousands of others did the same as us and we were just lucky that's all.'

'Maybe so but to travel all that way by horse and cart takes a great deal of courage it's something I couldn't do.'

'You would if you really had to Charles anyone would.'

Charles shook his head. 'Never not in a million years. Now there's something I'm curious about Petra now that you've sold your business what are your plans?'

Petra looked at him curiously, wondering how he find that out?'

'Well I've got a few things to sort out then I must look for some sort of work to pay the rent on our house.'

'That's odd, I thought somehow you owned it.' He paused a few moments. 'How would you like to come and work for me?'

Petra thought this rather a curious invitation from a man she knew very little about. 'In what sort of job Charles I'm not qualified at anything much?'

'Well with your experience in the food business and what I've seen of you so far would you like to be my housekeeper and personal assistant in my house in Belgrave Square?'

Petra looked at him in amazement this was something she hadn't quite expected and was he being serious as she had no previous knowledge of what a good housekeeper had to do.

'And what exactly would my duties be then?' She asked with a smile.

'Probably nothing more than you've been used to in your shop Petra just taking charge of the food supplies and making sure the other staff do their jobs properly. You will of course have your own flat upstairs with enough rooms for your children plus the use of my motor car and chauffeur whenever I'm not needing him.' He then paused a moment. 'How many children have you got still living with you?'

'Only three but two are working with only Boris still at school.'

Charles looked thoughtful at this answer. 'The two working are no problem. The other one will have to go to a local school but there are plenty of really good ones close by the house.'
Petra looked worried at this answer. 'But aren't they all very expensive around there?'

'Don't worry Petra whatever the fees are I'll pay them.'

Petra certainly looked interested at this proposal. 'What sort of salary are you offering?'

Charles paused a moment 'Well my last housekeeper was paid five pounds a week plus her food and flat how does that sound?

Petra quickly added her outgoings up and this sounded like a good offer one she really aught to take a chance on.

'That seems very good but first can I look at the house and have a few days to think about it Charles it is after all a bit unexpected and I'll have to talk to the children about it.'

'Do that and I'd love to meet your other children.'

'I can't see them not wanting to go.' She replied.

'What about this weekend then. How will that suit you?'

'Yes of course.' She replied. 'But I'll telephone you if I can't make it. What about your wife, does she approve of all this?'

Charles shook his head. 'No I'm not married so that's no problem so you will be sole charge of the London house at all times.'

Petra looked more than happy at the fact that Charles wasn't married. That was something that could have been a problem but she had the sneaking feeling that he might have other ideas about her. On the other hand he seemed to have checked up on her enough to be sure that she'd be suitable for the job.

When the weekend came the visit to Charles's house was a great success and Petra was amazed at the size of it, to her it was like a huge palace with a fantastic wide marble staircase, the like of which she'd only seen in Hollywood films. The children just couldn't believe their luck that they were going to get rooms so large and the fact that the house was so near to Hyde Park and the west end shops.

Within just a few short weeks the family had moved house and had settled comfortably into the upstairs flat. The two girls carried on working as usual and Boris was installed in a nearby school the only drawback was the cost of the new uniform for him. Petra found the job quite easy as the staff were all pleasant and kept the house very clean and tidy. In her spare off duty time Petra went for walks in Hyde Park and the west end visiting shops she'd never been in before and the occasional visit to a theatre was a bonus.

At the end of the first month Petra felt more confident about the job and not only were the household accounts simple but her contact with the staff always friendly and firm. Charles seemed more than pleased with the way things were going and he decided to have a chat with her regarding his future plans. He called her into his study late one afternoon once seated she nervously waited to hear what he wanted her for he obviously wanted to say something quite important.

'Well Petra you seem to have settled down quite well here all the staff speak well of you and things are running smoother than they have ever done before. So I have decided to make you another offer you don't have to decide at this moment whether to accept but think very carefully before you let me know your answer.'Petra looked curious perhaps this was leading up to a proposal of marriage but that would be crazy after all she'd only known him a few short months

'What is it Charles that you want me to do?'

Charles looked a little nervous at this point. 'Well something has come up that I aught to tell you about there is a chance that I might be appointed Lord Mayor of London very soon, and it is being whispered around that I should be married to take the job or at least to have a lady accompany me to attend all the functions.'

Petra looked very puzzled at this. 'Are you proposing marriage then Charles?'

'No sorry! He replied looking very uncomfortable. 'It's just that if I made you a large clothing allowance you'd come with me on some of my engagements.'

Petra felt a little more relaxed now that intentions were a little clearer so she paused a moment before answering. 'This is rather sudden and I am very flattered if that's the correct word that you'd want me to do this Charles but are you sure that I'm capable of carrying this off?'

'Of course you are, otherwise I wouldn't be asking you to do it. You'd be a stunning person to be with, anyway think about it there's no hurry.'

Petra couldn't help feeling a bit nervous about this possible new twist to her job and wondered just what the children would think about it that's if she decided to do it and tell them.

'Alright Charles! I'll think it over and probably let you know tomorrow then.'

This seemed to satisfy Charles that at least she hadn't said no so all he had to do was to wait for her answer not many women in his life so far had moved him in a way she did, plus she was a most beautiful person to be with and had the personality to carry this task off successfully. She must have been stunning twenty years ago and one of the most sought after girls in her village in Russia. He wished that at this moment, he had the courage to ask her to marry him but he wouldn't rush things and perhaps frighten her off. At least he'd prepared her for a better life than she'd had in the past.

Chapter Twenty Two

High Society

A few weeks later the appointment of Charles as Lord Mayor was announced and Petra having accepted Charles's offer had visited several west end clothing establishments for suitable wear. Gossip was rife as to who this good looking woman was going around with him and nobody seemed to know who she was and where she came from. Pictures were in all of the daily newspapers of them both when they were seen out together they certainly looked a happy pair together. When they'd completed a few engagements Petra casually asked Charles what qualifications and payment he received for doing this extra work. He laughed and told her it was an honour to be asked to do it and it would cost him a small fortune for only one season in office. This seemed very odd to her that someone should have to pay to do it what a funny country this was.

It was some months later after the finish of Mikael's term in Paris and he was home that Charles suggested that they all visit his country house in Buckinghamshire for a few days, Petra wondered why he wanted them to go there as that part of his life was unknown to her just what were his motives for it? The answer to this was soon revealed when Charles told her what he had in mind.

'The reason that I want you to come to my country house Petra is that whilst I was away last week I visited your son's college in Paris to check on his progress, and was astonished to find that he's progressed past my wildest expectations. Some of his work is as good as any ever produced by any pupil over the last fifty years.
Petra looked puzzled. 'And what is this to do with us seeing your other house then Charles?'

'Well at this moment I am restoring a lot of it and there is a section of the main dining room ceiling that would look great with religious murals covering it, and I would like Mikael to do the job for me of course I'd pay him well for it.'

'And if he agreed how do you know he'd be capable of doing it then?' Charles nodded and smiled. 'I've looked at similar work that he's done at college and it's fantastic.'

'How long would it take to complete then?' Asked Petra.

'Probably about a year roughly but not until he finishes his third year in Paris I wouldn't dream of taking him away from that.'
Petra looked astonished at this surely her son wasn't that good, or was he?'

'Which painting did you see of his then?' She asked.

'It was a religious mural similar to the one in the Sistine Chapel in Rome.' He replied. 'It was as though he'd taken a photograph of it and copied it. Of course I questioned his tutor about it but he'd only seen it in a book in the college library.'

'And are you willing to wait for him to do this to your house then?'

'Yes I am And somehow I think he may also exceed my expectations in two years time when I shall check his results very carefully.'
Petra just couldn't believe it she knew her son was talented but this was amazing. She wondered how he would take this when he found out what was being planned for his future.

'I do hope you are right about this. It's an awful risk on your part as anything could happen in the next two years,but he is a good boy and seems to want to be an artist so very badly.'

Charles smiled at her and nodded in agreement. 'Yes I am right he is a very talented boy and has a very bright future just as long as he doesn't fall into bad habits in Paris as some do, it can be a very distracting place for the young my dear.'

So when the week-end arrived the whole family journeyed by car to the house in Buckinghamshire where they were astonished at the size of the place. On their arrival they were introduced to the servants and then taken to their rooms where the children stood open mouthed at the size of these, even Belgrave Square seemed small to these.

During the first evening Petra questioned Charles about the wisdom of saying anything to Mikael so early especially as he'd only so far finished a complete year in Paris.

Charles was however very confident about the boy. 'He has performed extremely well so far and with another year under his belt he will be ready to perhaps make a small start on a bit of the painting, but anyway tomorrow I'll show him the job and see what he has to say about it. Petra eyed him in disbelief. 'Are you sure? It's a huge job for someone so young.'

'Of course I am right and he will be up to the task.' Said Charles. And some of his present work is as large as this and impressive as this will be.' Petra went to bed that night worried that this move might not be as easy as Charles thought and she lay awake for quite some time thinking about the coming day.

It was mid morning the next day that Charles invited them to look around the house before lunch and during this Mikael quietly asked his mother the reason for this visit. Petra said that Charles was on the board of governors at his old school and was interested in his work in Paris after receiving good reports about his work there. This answer seemed to satisfy Mikael so he and Petra followed Charles around the rest of the house as he explained each and every room in detail, he also told them the dates and artists names on every painting.

When they came finally to the main dining hall which was in a state of renovation Charles pointed to the huge centre ceiling area and looked at Mikael.

'What do you think we should do with that ceiling Mikael? It looks a bit bare doesn't it?'

Mikael stood there thoughtfully staring at the ceiling for quite some time before answering.

'It needs something different on it in keeping with the rest of the house sir maybe a large religious mural, it certainly looks very bare at the moment.'

Charles nodded in agreement. 'How would you like to do it then Mikael?'

The boy stood there thoughtfully staring at the ceiling. 'What makes you think that I can do such a thing?'

'If your work is as good in Paris at the end of next year as it is at present then the job is yours and that's a promise, I can wait to have the rest of the work in here done until you are finished.' Petra looked at Mikael to see his reaction to all this wondering if it wasn't all too much for him to take in all at once he really didn't look too happy but perhaps it hadn't quite sunk in yet.

'I need a little time to think about all this sir.' He said 'Perhaps if you gave me the measurements of the part you want painted then I could plan it better.'

Charles nodded this sounded much more positive at least he hadn't said no or he couldn't do it. 'I will get one of my men to do it for you before you go home Mikael then perhaps you can do me a rough sketch of what you propose sometime in the next few months.'
Mikael stood there deep in thought for a few minutes. 'I really would like to stay in this room on my own for a short while just to get the feel of the place, it's got a strange atmosphere as though something really important happened in here long ago.'

Charles looked at him in amazement. How on earth could this young boy have known the history of this place and how was he going to explain the centuries of intrigue that had taken place in these rooms.

'There have been tales about the owners of this house years ago and some of the servants swore that they'd seen ghosts and heard strange noises at night, but not since I've lived here.'

They left Mikael alone in the room until he was satisfied the scheme was at least possible and he made a few notes about the room.

The following day Petra thanked Charles for having them for the weekend before leaving for London on the train and Mikael seemed enthusiastic to have been given such a task. He asked his mother just why he of all people had been picked for the job? She then at this point decided to come clean about the whole thing and told him the whole story. He seemed quite pleased that someone should take such an interest in him and this seemed to remind him of an incident recently in Paris.

'Something strange happened one day last term after one of the lectures mother by quite a famous artist. His name was Chagal, he said that he'd painted father years ago before the war when he was connected with the opera company. He seemed so sad when I told him that he'd been killed in the war but pleased that he'd met me after all these years, and the fact that I was also a painter really impressed him. He guessed who I was because of my Russian name he also seemed very interested that I painted murals.'

Petra seemed pleased at this. How fortunate for him to have met such an artist even she knew how famous Chagal had now become she wondered if he'd ever finished the picture of her late husband, she also wondered if Mikael would become as good a painter as her Ivan was a dancer? This was something she'd have to wait for a few years yet but the signs were there all right only time would tell. The other children were also doing very well Anna had been promoted to export manager by her boss and the firm had grown enormously in size since she'd joined it. Nika was now in her second year as an apprentice dressmaker in a famous west end fashion house and loving every minute of it. Boris was also getting on well at his new school with top marks every term he was also a big help to Petra around the house in his spare time. He also was becoming quite friendly with Charles's chauffeur Thomas, who drove him to school each day and his son James who was about the same age as himself.

It was some months later that Mikael came home at the end of term and showed Petra sketches for Charles's ceiling hoping not only that she'd approve of them but also pass them on to him, he was slightly nervous to do this himself. She took them upstairs to the privacy of her own bedroom to study them and once alone she spread them out on the bed to look at them carefully. They were just as she expected quite stunning and for what were supposed to be just rough sketches they were perfect in colour and very detailed, they were as good as anything that she'd seen in any art gallery. She wrapped them up excitedly and noticed that both her hands were shaking and on looking in the mirror her face glowed with the pride and happiness that she felt inside.

That evening when Charles came home from the bank Petra took the sketches to his study and handed them to him nervously.

'Mikael is home and has brought these for you to look at.' She said.

Charles took them from her and smoothed them out on the desk he studied them carefully with a hint of a smile on his face.

'This calls for a celebration Petra and confirms my faith in your son these are even better than I expected at this stage of his progress we must take him out for a meal soon and I must buy him a small present for doing these amazing sketches.'

Petra looked slightly worried at this suggestion. 'That's nice but only if it's a quieter and smaller place than The Savoy Charles.'

Chapter Twenty Three

The Ceiling

It was in June the following year that Mikael started work in earnest on the ceiling of the dining hall at the house in Buckinghamshire, the room had been prepared beforehand for him with really sound scaffolding and ladders erected ready for his start. The ceiling had been thoroughly inspected by a surveyor who advised the use of suitable plywood to avoid future cracks in the surface of the ceiling. Charles had driven from London with him and instructed the staff to attend to his every need during his stay there. He told Mikael to take his time and not to rush the job. There were small sections of the ceiling that needed attention but they were quite a long way off the area he was going to start on. Charles made a point of telling Mikael that on no account was he to work long hours and tire himself out and that he'd be back the following weekend to see how he was getting on.

The week went well apart from a few small patches on the ceiling being slightly different from the rest but when the paint was applied they matched the rest of it. Of course Mikael's back and legs ached badly but this was to be expected as he'd never painted anything from such a position before, and every time he descended the ladder for meal breaks he stood there studying and admiring his work.

By the weekend he'd covered about two foot in length and was constantly checking the space to make sure his finished work would cover the ceiling equally, there had to be no room for error on his part. The edges of the ceiling he'd planned to leave blank in order to paint some sort of framework to give it a better effect. The colours were stunning and looked even better from below and the staff were quietly viewing the transformation at every opportunity they'd obviously never seen anything like this done before. By Saturday lunchtime he was nervously awaiting the arrival of Charles and for him to give an opinion on the work so far.

Mikael was getting cleaned up when Charles arrived so he didn't see him go straight to the dining hall and stand staring at the ceiling for quite some time, the look on his face said it all, here was pure genius indeed the boy was truly a great painter. At lunch he was all smiles and felt he had to praise Mikael without seeming to overdo things.

'You certainly are making a good job of the ceiling Mikael and don't think for one moment that you are doing it all a bit slowly it's all going extremely well so far so don't spoil it.'

Mikael looked a bit nervous at this remark. 'Yes I understand what you are saying and will bear it in mind. This is my first attempt at anything as big as this and I am of course a little frightened of spoiling it and having to start again.'

The following week things went a bit better for Mikael and he seemed to get a little more confident as time went by and by the end of the week he'd not only got three sections finished but was starting the fourth. The whole dining room was now beginning to take on a new atmosphere and appearance and certainly looked a lot brighter. He knew that there was only three more weeks left until the next term started in Paris so he had to make the best of the time left to him.

Back in London Petra was getting regular reports of Mikael's progress and couldn't wait to see just what he'd done since he first started work at the house. She hoped that he wasn't overdoing things and working too hard knowing just what a perfectionist he was almost like his father, and only his best was good enough. If he managed to complete this task to the standard that she expected of him this would be not only a fantastic achievement in itself but also a great start to his life as a young artist. She also hoped that this gift he'd been given wouldn't fade and that he'd be left with nothing to carry him forward in later life but at this stage things looked very promising.

At the end of his school holiday Mikael felt more than satisfied with his achievement and with a reasonable amount finished now looked forward to coming back during the Christmas break to do another section of the ceiling, at this point of the job he certainly felt more confident than he'd ever been. On the last night Charles came with his mother to take him back to London but before leaving they all had a celebration dinner in the house in recognition of his efforts there, both Charles and Petra were well pleased with what he'd done. At this point Charles gave him a cheque for the first part of the job and Mikael thanked him and said it was the first piece of serious money that he'd ever earned and he was so very happy. Once back in college Mikael was slightly restless and didn't seem to be able to concentrate as well as before. his tutor noticed this and decided to find out the reason for this sudden change, he decided to question him about it.

'What did you do during your summer holiday Mikael?'
Mikael looked at him in surprise perhaps he shouldn't mention what he'd been up to but what did it matter the time was his own to do whatever he wanted. 'Oh not very much really but someone I know asked me to do some painting for him.'

'You mean house painting?' Said the tutor.

'No a ceiling mural in his dining room.'

'And did you finish it then?'

'No just a small part the rest will probably take about two years.'
The tutor looked surprised. 'And is he paying you for doing it then?'

'Of course! Replied Mikael. Otherwise I wouldn't do it.'
The tutor paused a moment this was something he hadn't heard of before but it certainly was very interesting knowing just how good an artist this boy was he decided to question him further.

'Have you got a sketch of what you did then?'

Mikael nodded. 'A small part, would you like to see it then?'

'Of course because if it's any good the management have a scheme that awards a prize for the best ideas each term and occasionally every few years they exhibit the most exceptional work in the Hall of Fame.'
Mikael smiled with satisfaction at this. He thought his tutor was going to be annoyed at having worked in the holiday time.

'Would you really like me to show it you then?' He said.

'Very much I'll wait here while you get it Mikael.'

After a few minutes Mikael returned with the sketch and the tutor studied it for quite some time. 'This is really astounding Mikael. Where did you get this idea from?'

'Oh I suppose reading books of religious paintings.'

The tutor nodded this was by far the best piece of work by a young student that he'd ever seen and he couldn't wait to show this to his superiors.

'Can I borrow this for a while to show it to the managers?'

'Of course if you want to anyway I've got another one in my room.'

'You've got another.... like this?' Said the tutor in amazement.

Mikael nodded. 'It's slightly different but nearly as good.'

The tutor looked amazed that one sketch like this was an achievement in itself but two was beyond belief he left the room with mixed feelings in all his years at the college he'd never seen such detailed work from a student.

It was some days later that Mikael was summoned to the headmasters study to be interrogated about his sketch as so far there seemed to be a difference of opinion as to whether he'd actually done it or not.

'Sit down Mikael.' Said the head picking up the sketch. Mikael did as he was told nervously.'

'This painting that you gave your tutor, is it really your own work, you didn't copy it from a book did you?'

'No sir! You won't find it in any books it's something I worked out myself over time.'

The headmaster looked sternly at him. 'So if I gave you a piece of paper you cold sketch me something similar then?' 'Yes I think so.'

The headmaster smiled. 'Alright then have a go on this.' He passed him a pad and a pencil and sat back in anticipation still very sceptical. Mikael started to draw a few lines slowly then as the minutes ticked by the headmaster quietly glanced through the mornings newspaper.

It was almost an hour when Mikael suddenly stopped work and put the pencil down on the desk the relief showing on his face doing something like this with someone watching had been a bit nerve racking. But now it was over and the result was quite satisfying he glanced at it casually before passing it over to the headmaster to look at. This was the moment of truth would the drawing stand up to his scrutiny and be as good as the first effort ? The look on the headmasters face was a picture in itself. This boy was a true genius indeed and nothing they could teach him would really further improve his skill as an artist. What could he now say to this boy without spoiling what was a likeable self effacing person who probably didn't realise his true full potential.

'Well Mikael this is quite a lot better than I really expected of you at this stage of your course with us and despite being obviously a little nervous doing this in front of me you have really excelled yourself. So much so that I am going to give you not only the opportunity of putting something on our Wall of Fame, but also telling you that to my way of thinking you are the most outstanding pupil this college had had for many years and will inform your sponsor and mother that after this term ending you will need no further lessons from us.'

The headmaster then stood up and shook Mikaels hand warmly. 'I will inform the tutor to supervise your work in the Hall of Fame for us and am certain the result will be something quite outstanding.'
Mikael left the room feeling elated this was indeed something he hadn't really expected. Now he could concentrate on finishing his work at Charles's house, plus he would soon be free to do other things at his leisure.

The next few weeks passed very quickly and Mikael completed his small mural in the Hall of Fame in the college and it didn't look out of place there, it was equally as good of most of the other exhibits on display and   one of the few signed by a Russian artist he was certainly proud of his work.

Chapter Twenty Four

Back Home

Once back home Mikael spent his first week resting and getting used to living in England once again before being taken to Buckinghamshire to carry on with his work there. Charles although slightly disappointed that he hadn't finished the whole course in Paris was also very impressed at the glowing report from the headmaster about Mikael, not only his work but the mural as well this was an outstanding achievement in itself left there for future generations to see. It was going to be a completely different life for him from now on no longer living to set rules and achievement targets set by others, from now on his future was in his own hands and this year was going to be make or break for him.

It all looked completely different as he stood on the scaffold in the dining room looking at the work he'd already completed. Now he really could take his time and achieve absolute perfection, with nothing else to think about but his painting and enjoying living in the peace of the countryside. Odd moments were spent talking to the staff and finding out about their lives in general he was very impressed with the way they all went about their duties but couldn't understand why it took so many of them to run the place. Surely some of the work could be done by less staff and little did he know that what he learned there was to come in handy one day in his own life.

All was well with the work until late one evening just as Mikael was feeling a bit tired he had the feeling that someone was standing behind him on the scaffolding. A soft voice almost hardly audible said very abruptly. (That bit's not quite right do it again)

Mikael turned around startled fearing it might be one of the ghosts that had been seen about the place, but all he saw was an outline of an old man's face peering at him in the space between him and the wall. The apparition vanished as quickly as it had come and Mikael stood there shaking, what did the old man mean and what was wrong with his work? He decided to have a closer look at it maybe it wasn't as good as usual. He laid down his brushes and moved closer to the mural as the light was beginning to fade a little there was a slight brush stroke too many in one corner but he would have noticed it anyway sometime later.

The following week he decided to ask Charles about this strange apparition on the scaffold and find out who it might have been, it was obviously someone familiar with painting. He described in great detail the man's face who had very long grey hair and a beard to match. Charles listened to the description then wanted to know more about the incident.

'Has anything like this happened to to you before Mikael?' He asked.'

'No never!' Replied Mikael without hesitation.

Charles looked slightly worried at this then walked across the room to the open library and came back with an old dusty book he opened it and shielding half the page showed it to Mikael.
'Is this person something like what you saw then Mikael?'

Mikael studied the picture a moment and nodded. 'Yes that's him alright. Did he live here then?'

Charles smiled and shook his head. 'No not to my knowledge this man died a few hundred years ago his name was Michelangelo and it seems he has taken an interest in what you are doing here. Are you sure you've never seen this picture before?'

'No. Should I have?'

Charles wondered if the boy had come across this somewhere in the college in Paris but he seemed reasonably honest in his answer.
'Well let me know if it happens again perhaps it was just a one off or you were a bit on the tired side that evening.

Charles decided to let the matter rest perhaps the boy had been visited by a spirit of the past, he had heard of writers who said they had been inspired by long dead novelists and found themselves able to write in an uncanny similar style.

Glancing up at the ceiling Charles studied carefully Mikael's latest addition to his work and then walked up and down admiring it, from, the smile on his face it was evident to Mikael that he liked what he saw. 'This is really magnificent Mikael. You must be really proud of yourself at achieving this result?'

Mikael dipped his brushes in cleaner and wiped them on a cloth.

'Yes it's a nice feeling every time I look up at it, but the finish seems such a long way off perhaps as long as another nine months.'

'Don't worry Mikael time is not important and anyway take a week off whenever you feel like it, I don't want you falling off the scaffold because you're tired.'

A few weeks later Mikael did decide to go home for a week to see his family and visit a few art galleries in London just to see what other artists works were like. His mother and the other children were happy to see him again but Petra noticed that he looked quite a lot thinner than when she'd last seen him and wondered if he'd been eating regularly. Charles assured her that the staff at the house made sure that he was well looked after at all times, and that his slight weight loss was down to climbing the scaffold a few times a day and stretching to reach the ceiling. Petra seemed to accept this explanation but still didn't like the pale look and bony look of her son he certainly never looked like that before. Before Mikael went back to the country he seemed to have picked up a bit and lost his slightly worried look, Petra still packed him a few goodies to take back just in case he was missing some of the food he normally had at home.

Once back at the big house Mikael got back in routine again and seemed to speed up a bit. Whether this was due to the rest he'd had or that he could see how much progress he was now making, the fact was he could see the end of the job was in sight. On his next visit Charles was so pleased with the way things were going that he decided to invite some of his close friends to stay the weekend to give their opinion on the so far completed work.

This turned out to be a good move as one of them turned out to be a friend of an Ambassador who wanted a similar piece of work doing in his London dining room. Charles although pleased at this reaction had to explain that Mikael couldn't possibly start such a task for quite some time as he'd first have to accept and have a rest after finishing this one. After the guests had left Charles told Mikael about this but warned him that it might not happen and not to count on it too much.

It was six months later that the painting was finally finished and a happy Mikael packed his things and went home to London, the house painters moved in and started to finish the rest of the dining room. Charles was in a very happy mood and congratulated Mikael on his fantastic achievement. The result was far better than could ever have been imagined, he resolved to help Mikael gain more experience by giving him a small task once they got back to town.

The following week Charles called Mikael into his library to test him out and see just what his reaction would be, once inside Charles took a picture down from the wall and handed it to him.

'What's wrong with this picture Mikael?' He asked.

Mikael studied it intensely for quite some time before answering.'It has been hung in a sunny place sometime and become a little faded on the edges.'

Charles nodded smiling. 'Quite right Mikael and do you think that you could restore it to it's rightful condition?'

'Yes I hope so but it might take a couple of weeks.'

'Then the job's yours and if you do it as I think you will then we will start on the next stage of your artistic education, we will both go to some fine art auctions. This will give you an insight to what sort of a living can be made out of buying and selling good quality pictures. It can be very lucrative if you make the right decisions.'

This sounded like a very interesting change in his way of life and Mikael was flattered that Charles should take so much interest in his future.

'I'm very grateful for all you've done for me Charles and hope that someday I can repay you in some way for your kindness. I'd really look forward to seeing an auction of paintings with you, that would be a very exiting thing to watch.'

'That's settled then. Take the painting and see what you can do with it for me we'll go to the auction next week together.'

Mikael went back upstairs to his room to study the painting more closely and decide just how to restore it as carefully as possible so as to bring it back to it's original state, he just knew he could do it but it would take time that's all.

Chapter Twenty Five

The Offer

The next few months went well for Mikael with his knowledge of painting, auctions, and restoring increasing daily, so much so that he very soon was renting a small studio in Chelsea in partnership with another young painter. He was also gaining a reputation as a very competent restorer and had a quite large list of clients that brought him a steady trickle of work which kept him reasonably busy. He was at last approached by a diplomat from the Russian Embassy to work on a ceiling painting in their building in central London, he told the man that he'd let him know if it was possible. As this might turn out to be a long drawn out job Mikael decided to ask Charles what he should do and the chances of not being paid for such a task

He told him that he aught to ask for a reasonable fee before taking on the job, roughly a quarter of the the final sum, so that should they not pay the rest at least he'd have the satisfaction of knowing it would advertise his work to most of the countries of the world. Mikael took this advice and went one better and asked for half the fee in advance after viewing the house which although very stylish, some parts looked a bit neglected.

The first secretary he met and who sanctioned the project quizzed him at great length before agreeing everything and was pleasantly surprised at finding him so young and the son of a Russian dancer, this seemed to clinch the interview most decidedly and he gave Mikael the cheque for half the final amount. They had obviously gone into his past work and had been given the right recommendations now all Mikael had to do was get them to set up the scaffolding and ladders to suit him. This they promised to get ready for the following week and Mikael left the Embassy full of confidence in himself and eager to start work on it. On the way home he couldn't help taking the cheque out of his pocket to remind himself of what he'd just achieved, it was to him an amazing result.

Back home he related what had happened to his mother step by step how the interview had gone and Petra stood there smiling with satisfaction, she could hardly believe that he'd become so business like so quickly and felt very proud of him. He'd certainly grown up a lot in the last year and was taking on a lot of his fathers quiet confidence and he seemed very sure of himself at all times.

Petra herself seemed to have settled into her job very well and knew that Charles was pleased with the way she was running the house he was also constantly praising her in front of his many close friends. She now felt sure that she had a job for life as long as things stayed as they were but often wondered what would happen if he were to get married, but there was no sign of that happening at present. He was always very polite in his dealings with her more so when other household staff were present, it was as though he didn't want them to feel that he was treating her better than them.

It was much later that year when things began to change a little and Petra noticed that Charles started by asking her whether she was satisfied with her role in the house. She was a little puzzled about his motive for asking such a question especially as he had quite a smile on his face.

'Of course I am.' She replied. 'Life is good here and the children are very happy living here.'

Charles moved a little closer and paused a moment before speaking.

'You have really changed the way this house is run Petra and my life has been made so much easier since you came here, so much so that I'd find it hard to run my life without you.'

Petra looked at him wondering just what he was getting at what was this leading up to she thought? What he said next took her almost completely by surprise even though there had been moments when she thought he had been a little over friendly towards her. 'For quite some time I've been watching how you go about your job here Petra and I have really admired the way you seem to fit in this way of life, especially when important people visit us.' He paused as though unsure of what to say next.

'What would you say if I asked you to marry me Petra?'

She looked at him in amazement not knowing what to say this was a very unexpected statement from him.

'That's a very strange way of putting it. Are you seriously proposing to me then?' She said.

Charles nodded smiling. 'Of course I am Petra do you want me to say it all properly then?'

Petra still wasn't convinced that he was serious about it but felt she needed time to think it over after all she'd never heard of anyone rich marrying their housekeeper before. 'This is really unexpected Charles what will the other servants say about it when they find out?'

'They shan't unless you say yes then it won't matter much anyway.'

Petra moved towards the window and glanced out wondering just what to say next she could feel her heart pounding quite rapidly.

'Would you mind if I took a few days to think about this Charles especially as I have the children to think of as well?'

'Of course my dear take your time and if your answer is yes the children will be well provided for and I will treat them as mine they really are a pleasure to live with.'

'Thank you Charles. They all think a lot of you and say you are a very kind man. Life has been so much better here than they have had before, they all especially like being so close to the park and the marvellous shops.'

'Good. That's settled then go away and seriously think about what I've said, and I do hope that you accept as I'm very much in love with you and have been for quite some time now.'

Petra's hands shook a little as she turned to leave the room, this was indeed something she'd not expected, what would the children have to say when she finally told them.

Back in her own room she sat down to recover a little she really didn't love the man but was more than fond of him as he'd always treated her well, perhaps she might in time grow to love him, she'd read that in books.

She picked up the framed photo of Ivan her dear dead husband and wondered what he would have thought about it all? He would probably say go for it Petra what have you got to lose it's bound to turn out all right. This was just the moment to have a glass of brandy to calm herself down and bring her back to normality. She hadn't committed herself to anything yet and their was work to do before the children came home. Later the house had suddenly changed as she moved around it and even the sun seemed brighter as it shone through the windows, life could be so unpredictable. She tried to picture herself as the lady of the house and wondered if she'd still be as happy as she was at this moment in time or would the pressure of the extra responsibilities be too much?

After thinking about it all for quite some days Petra decided to give Charles the answer whilst all the children were out and knocked on his study door quietly, hearing him answer she opened the door and walked in.

'Oh hello Petra! Do sit down I hope you've got good news for me?'

Petra sat on a nearby chair and looked very seriously at him.

'Well I think so Charles that is if you want the answer I'm going to give you.'

Charles looked a little puzzled what could she mean by that he thought?

'Then just what is your answer then?'

Petra looked slightly nervous and was hoping what she was about to tell him wouldn't upset him.

'I've decided to accept your kind proposal of marriage Charles but I just have to make it very clear that although I think a lot of you I really don't love you, though perhaps things may change when we get to know each other better.'

Charles's face lit up at this statement and he moved quickly towards her and kissed her lightly on the cheek. 'Thank you Petra for that very honest answer it has made my day that you have accepted I think that you are a most wonderful person and I love you dearly, this calls for a celebration drink you have made me very happy.'

He moved towards the cupboard and brought back two glasses and a bottle of champagne then having opened it poured it out and handed Petra one.

'Cheers Petra And may we have many happy years together.'

Petra raised her glass and sipped the drink still quite nervously and wondering if she was doing the right thing, she certainly hoped so telling the children was going to be the next big hurdle.

Chapter Twenty Six

The Wedding

When the children were finally told they were all overjoyed that their mother should be doing such a thing, and once they discovered that they could soon move downstairs to bigger rooms this was indeed a bonus. Suddenly they all felt as though their world was about to change even though they were unaware of the future plans that Charles had in store for them. Petra wanted the wedding to be kept as quiet as possible mainly due to her having been married already in a catholic church. Charles agreed and only invited very close friends to the registry office and reception at the London house, but despite trying to keep it slightly secret word soon got out and the telephone never stopped ringing with well wishers congratulating him on the event.

The week before the wedding Petra decided to have a serious talk to Charles about their relationship and clear the air regarding her real feelings for him, she was more than a little nervous about the forthcoming marriage and her role as wife to a man owning two very large properties. Although she had managed to look after the staff and control the finances of the London house for quite some time the prospect of looking after the country house was a daunting one she didn't want, this was well beyond anything she'd want to experience it was a completely different world.

He was in the library sitting reading as she entered after knocking as she always did and as she entered Charles could tell by her face that she looked a little troubled.

'What's wrong Petra?' He said quietly.

'It's just that there are a few things I have to know before the wedding, things we haven't really discussed properly and I'm a little worried about them that's all.'

'Well tell me what they are then my dear?'

Petra nervously sat near him and started with what she thought was the simplest problem. 'It's the running of the country house for a start. It's much bigger than this one and I'm really worried that I've no experience of such a large building as this one.'

Charles smiled, if this was the only worry she had it was an easy question to answer, he put his book down hoping this was her only fear.

'Don't worry about that at all Petra. Everything out there is under control and I have enough staff there to look after the place very competently besides I go there regularly enough to supervise how it's being run. So all you have to worry about is this house and I've already advertised for a house keeper for this house.'

Petra looked a little relieved at this answer she then thought about the next problem worrying her.

'As this has all been a bit sudden for me Charles would you mind if we didn't sleep together for a little while after we get married as that side of it really worries me a bit?'

'I'm glad you said that Petra. I also am slightly nervous and that's why I've half arranged a trip to Paris for us if that's alright with you?'

Petra's face brightened at this perhaps now she could visit her relations again there and with twin beds in a hotel that might solve the problem she faced.

'Yes I'd love to go to Paris Charles.'

'Right then! That's settled now I can confirm the booking and I've opened an account for you at all the Knightsbridge stores to buy whatever clothes you need in future, and there's no need to worry about what they cost I want you looking your best at all times.'

Petra got up and moved towards him bent down and kissed him on the cheek. 'Thank you for listening and being so kind Charles I'll go shopping tomorrow then and try and find some suitable clothes.

On the morning of the wedding the house was buzzing with activity and all the children were home for the day getting ready for the big event, Petra sat in front of her dressing table combing her hair whilst looking in the mirror. How on earth was she going to get through this day? Here she was about to marry a man she didn't love and shaking at the prospect of being in charge of a large house full of servants that to her seemed so wasteful. The only consolation was that for the first time in her life she and her children were now going to be financially secure for the rest of their lives. Glancing in the mirror her thoughts turned to the first time she'd seen those hungry looking children looking through her fish shop window. They waited patiently every night for any scraps of batter and left over chips hoping to get some, their mothers sent them knowing there was no money for food in the house whilst their husbands were down at the local pub squandering what little they had.

Petra glanced at the nearby clock there was less than two hours to go and then she'd be married to Charles Philips wealthy stockbroker and banker but would this make her any happier than she already was? Only time would tell. She finished dressing and went downstairs where the children were already waiting laughing and joking but as she reached the bottom stair they turned and gasped open mouthed. They'd never seen their mother dressed in such fine clothes and all gathered round to tell her how lovely she looked.

Upstairs Charles was nervously finishing dressing. His thoughts at this time were of just what he was getting into marrying his pretty housekeeper. Although he was absolutely sure it was the the best decision he'd ever made in his life he couldn't help wondering just what his friends really thought about it all. Some of them he felt really envied him because she was such a beauty and super efficient at whatever he'd asked her to do. But now was the time he dreaded most of all. Was it possible that Petra might change her mind and want to call it all off? He certainly hoped not as she seemed so happy these last few days as were all her children they were thrilled with the prospect of their mother being the lady of the house.

He waited until the car had left with the children before going downstairs to join Petra who was looking radiant with a serene smile on her face, he kissed her lightly on the cheek and gave her a warm hug.

'This is going to be one of the best days of my life.' He said. 'And I hope it makes you happy Petra?'

She looked at him thoughtfully and nodded. 'Yes of course I'm happy but not only for me but the children as well, they are thrilled.'

A few minutes later the car stopped outside ready for them to leave for the wedding ceremony as they both settled back in the car seats Petra glanced around to see if anyone had been watching, she was relieved to note that nobody was in sight. On arrival at Caxton Hall there were a few of Charles's close friends anxiously waiting to greet them and having done so they all went inside the building together.

The formal ceremony only lasted some twenty minutes and the happy couple left hand in hand followed by the children.An extra car was waiting outside for the children and the next stop was the reception laid on in the Square outside the house with a huge marquee erected on the lawn. The event wasn't planned to start until early evening so once having checked that everything was going smoothly Petra and Charles went back to the house to change and relax for a few hours knowing that they'd need all their energy to get them through the very hectic evening.

One thing that Petra had insisted on was that all the staff in the house should be invited to the evening's festivities as all the catering was being done by a large food store nearby. Charles although a little hesitant at first, agreed to this knowing that there might be a few snooty bankers wives who would certainly not approve of such goings on. Shortly before the first guests were due to arrive Charles and a very nervous Petra were there ready to greet them this was whispered to be one of the best parties of the year, and many of the richest people in London had been invited to the event. It seemed amazing how quickly the time passed for Petra once the first hundred guests had been greeted by them both, and by the time the queue had got down to a trickle they could relax a little and have a quiet drink with the children.

The band that had been engaged for the evening was really superb and had most of the guests on their feet when they were not in the food tent eating, the house staff were really enjoying it as well and didn't look a bit out of place. But sadly it all had to end eventually at well past midnight and they slowly made their way home across the road.

Petra had previously half made her mind up to sleep alone that first night but feeling really sorry for Charles, who had made such an effort with everything on the day, she changed her mind. But first of all, she warned him that due to the pressure of the days events and the fact that she was unusually tired she just might fall asleep very quickly. This didn't seem to bother him too much and he was happy that at least they'd be together the first night.

The following morning the children were very inquisitive about how Petra felt sleeping with someone who'd until recently been her employer but she brushed them off laughing and told them to mind their own business. She then spent the whole day preparing for the trip to Paris. This time she hoped it would be more of a holiday than the last time she'd gone there.

Chapter Twenty Seven

The Honeymoon

Paris was even better than Petra had ever known it the hotel was very grand and Charles had hired a large car and chauffeur for the duration of their stay, it was just like a dream that she would somehow wake up from. The view of the whole of the Champs Eleysees was a stunning sight to wake up with and a completely different world from the places she lived in previously in Paris.

They spent the first few days touring the city's famous places and dining in riverside restaurants, Charles had previously booked all the evenings with the best entertainment centres. The visit to the Paris Opera House was the icing on the cake for Petra which brought back memories of Ivan dancing there all those years ago. With all the luxury of her life now she felt there was still no comparison to the happiness of her previous life with Ivan and no matter what happened now she'd never pass a day without thinking about him.

When they'd been to almost every possible tourist site in the city Charles was ready to visit Petra's relations on the farm knowing that this would really please her. It was only a short journey by car and Petra was a little surprised and shocked at the difference to the appearance of the farm, it looked more run down than when she'd last seen it. When the car stopped outside the gate Yuri spotted them and walked cautiously forward before recognising Petra his face lit up at the sight of her and he rushed out to hug her.

'You should have told me you were coming Petra. This is a surprise.'

Petra laughed at this remark knowing that the farm had no telephone.

'This is my new husband Charles, Yuri, we were married last week.'

Yuri studied them both a second then shook Charles's hand warmly.

'Congratulations to you both. Come inside I'll call Olga, she will be very happy to see you.'

At that moment Olga appeared in the doorway and rushed towards Petra laughing and threw her arms around her.

'How good to see you again Petra. How are you?'

'Fine Olga and how are you all keeping?'

Olga's face changed a little. 'Well since you came last nasty things have happened. The man who owns this land wants to charge us a lot more rent and we cannot really afford it.' She glanced at Charles then at Petra curiously.

Petra realised that she forgotten to introduce Charles yet and knew how uncomfortable he must feel just standing there.

'This is my husband Charles, and we've not long been married.'

Olga nodded and smiled at Charles. 'That's nice but where are the children?'

'Oh they are in London. Replied Petra. 'And they are being well looked after there.'

Olga motioned towards the chairs. 'Do sit down and I'll bring some coffee for you both.'

After they'd finished coffee Charles asked Yuri if he could look around the farm which seemed like a good idea as he wanted to quiz him about the farm tenancy more. Once inside the largest barn and alone together Charles raised the subject with Yuri.

'How long have you been here then Yuri?'

Yuri paused to think about it a moment before answering.

'About nine years I think but it seems much longer.'

Charles looked thoughtful and his eyes were everywhere looking for signs of what he regarded as careful management.

'What would you say to a job in England if it were offered to you Yuri?'

'Doing what? I've only been a farmer all my life.'

Charles smiled. 'That is no problem the job that I have in mind would be farming on a small scale and living quarters for you and your family.' Yuri looked slightly puzzled at this offer this was totally unexpected especially from a complete stranger.

'But you don't know me, how can you offer me such a job?'

'Easily. I just know you'd be right for what I have in mind and it would please Petra to have you all living closer to her.'
Yuri still looked puzzled and wondered just what this man had in mind for him. ' Is it possible to come to England and look at this job you are offering me?'

'Of course you can! We will be going back in a few days and if you agree you can come with us.'

'Does Petra know about this?'

'No not yet, speak to your wife and if she likes the idea we'll then tell Petra.'

'Why are you doing this for us?'

'Because this is something Petra would want for you and after all we are family now aren't we?'

At this point Charles was beginning to find that speaking in his unfamiliar French a bit of a strain the few words that he used in the hotels were normally passable, so he suggested that they return to the house to talk to the wives.

Once back in the farmhouse they found the ladies discussing the problem of the farm rent so Charles suggested that Yuri take Olga to another room and tell her what they had just discussed.

Petra was curious to know just what was going on so Charles decided to tell her the bare facts hoping that she'd be pleased with the idea, to him it was only something that filled a gap in a plan he'd been working on for some time. He was aware that she looked slightly worried and was a very practical person who could probably see snags he'd not thought of but for now it was only a germ of an idea. 'Do you really have a job for him Charles?'

'Of course I have. There is a lot of land on my estate could be put to some good use and a few empty cottages as well they could live in. For quite some time I've thought about opening up the house to the public and to do it they'd need quite a lot of farm food to feed the extra staff needed.'

Petra sat there looking more interested now and wondering how long he'd had such plans without mentioning them to her, but then again she'd not shown much enthusiasm about the estate since being given the house to look after.

'What about their children Charles They might not want to move?'

'It would be a better life for them in England, Petra, I'm sure of that and from what you've already told me they are a hard-working family and should fit in well with my plans.'

Just then Yuri and Olga came back into the room full of smiles and Olga was the first to speak.

'You must both stay to supper Petra and listen while we tell the children what you've offered us and I'm sure that they will be very pleased especially as there isn't much of a future here for them at present.'

'Thank you.' Said Charles. 'You both sound as though you like the idea of a move and I promise we'll look after you.'

Later when supper was over Olga took the two children Natalya and Dimitri aside and broke the good news to them, They were very surprised and seemed to like the sound of the plan, but wanted a little time to get used to the idea. Whilst they were out of the room Charles brought up the question of possibly having to move their furniture to England but Yuri laughed and said it wasn't worth much and it would be cheaper to buy some more. By now Yuri was relishing the idea of going to England to check out the job that Charles had offered him and knew that the way things were on the farm he'd never make a go of it there.

It was decided that being so late Petra and Charles should stay the night in order to set off early the next morning with Yuri in order to give him time to pack. The chauffeur was given some money to find himself suitable lodgings for the night as there wasn't really enough room in the farmhouse for him as well.

The following morning was a busy time with all the family there to bid farewell to Yuri they had never been apart from each other ever before not even for a day. This to him was a great adventure going to another country with the prospect of another job on a farm he'd never seen, he sincerely hoped it would turn out better than the present one had. On arrival in Paris he was astonished at the size of it he'd only seen pictures of it before this and never dreamed he'd be staying in a posh hotel like this one. They left for England the next day and spent the following one in Belgrave Square before visiting Charles's country house which really impressed Yuri, and having explained the extent of the job Charles convinced him to take it and move from France.

Chapter Twenty Eight

Together again

The next few months were hectic ones for Petra who was slightly worried that the life in England might not suit Yuri and Olga but things seemed to work out well for them, and they soon settled down and both the children found work locally.

Married life was better than she had expected and even sleeping with Charles was not the problem that she had anticipated, every day she grew a bit fonder of him as he was such a kind and considerate man. She now wanted to take more of an interest in the country house now that her relations were living there and Charles was more than pleased with her change of mind. He now consulted her on every change he made and she seemed to come up with some very sound ideas that he'd never thought of. The most ambitious one being opening the gardens to the public at weekends this would help towards the upkeep of the property, and although Charles was a very rich man this huge mansion was quite a drain on his income.

As the lady of the house now Petra seemed to have quite a lot of time on her hands and Charles suggested that they socialized a bit more just to help her make friends, this seemed to work out alright but she found most of the rich people he mixed with a little stuffy and full of themselves. There was one very nice woman from an Arab Embassy who seemed more than interested in Mikael's work and wanted her husband the ambassador to have him do some work at their residence for them. She had seen some of his works in other places and really liked them, they seemed to her the nearest of their kind to the works in the Vatican in Rome.

Within weeks her husband had contacted Mikael and he'd started work on the ceiling in their residence dining room and knew that the finished piece would be seen by Ambassador's from around the world. He had great hopes that this would probably bring in much more work in the months ahead. This proved to be the case as when he'd finished the work he got a call from the Italian Embassy to do a much larger ceiling painting for them. It was whilst working there that he became very friendly with the Ambassador's eldest daughter Rosa and spent many hours talking to her mainly when her parents were absent.

When they found out that their daughter was speaking to Mikael and wanted to see him outside of the home they insisted that she be escorted always with a senior member of the house staff. This was not what Rosa wanted or expected as other girls in her college had much more freedom than this and she rebelled, but to no avail, her parents would not give way on this rule.

After many months of seeing each other almost weekly the two of them were growing very attached so much so that the ambassador decided to have a quiet chat with Mikael to find out his intentions towards his daughter. He didn't want to frighten him off in any way as he really liked the boy and felt he was unusually talented this was just to make sure this was not a youthful flirtation in any way. He arranged to speak with Mikael one afternoon when Rosa would not be around and in the privacy of his study. He sat waiting at his desk with a list of questions in front of him when Mikael knocked and entered the room, the ambassador looked up nodded and motioned him to be seated.

'Thank you for coming Mikael. There is something I wish to speak to you about and you probably know just what it is?'

Mikael looked very nervous. 'I think so sir. Is it about Rosa?'

'Yes of course. You both seem to be seeing rather a lot of each other lately?'

Mikael nodded. 'Yes we have.'

The ambassador looked serious. 'Well I really need to know a bit more about you if you intend seeing her again. Of course I checked out your past academic qualifications before giving you work in my house,and they were first class, but this is something quite different and I'd like to know first of all your ambitions for the future?'

Mikael suddenly felt a bit more at ease. If this man had checked his past out and seemed satisfied then he'd tell him just what was capable of.

'Well sir at the moment as you know I'm earning much more than most artists of my age plus I'm a very competent picture restorer and I buy and sell a lot at fine art auctions.'

The ambassador looked surprised at this statement this was not what he'd expected at this point and there was a hint of a smile on his face.

'You surprise me Mikael I didn't know that much about you and from what you say you probably earn almost as much as I do?'

Mikael grinned at this. 'No I don't think so. I've also checked on you and you are a successful businessman in your own right, I also know that to do your job you have to be someone special as well.'

The ambassador nodded. 'Yes of course and mixing with others from different countries it helps to also speak a few languages, how many besides English do you speak Mikael?'

Mikael thought for a few seconds. 'French, German, Italian, Russian, and just a little Polish as well.' he replied.

The interview seemed to be going well for Mikael and the ambassador was beginning to run out of questions for the time, and so he decided to give Mikael the benefit of doubt and just give him a little warning about courting his daughter.

'Well Mikael you seem to be quite an intelligent and resourceful young man and although you have my permission to see my daughter whenever it suits you do not harm her in any way. For if you do your prospects of making a living here or anywhere else in the world will be very limited, I would see to that so be careful and treat her well. If by chance your relationship with her grows further you will see that she's got very expensive tastes and won't want to live a life of poverty in any way. Do you understand what I'm saying?'

Mikael nodded nervously wanting this to be over quickly he hadn't thought his friendship with Rosa had reached that sort of stage yet. Perhaps he'd better tread carefully in future, he couldn't afford to upset this man at all. Besides they'd barely got beyond the goodnight kiss stage so far with someone watching their every move.

'Yes I do understand you sir and promise to look after Rosa at all times.'

The ambassador moved to stand up he then held out his hand towards Mikael and shook it. 'Thank you Mikael I think we understand each other quite well now and I hope I never have to mention such things again to you.'

Mikael left the room slightly relieved and outside felt glad to have survived the interview.

The following day whilst he was out with Rosa in the adjoining square Mikael mentioned his encounter with her father and she smiled and they then moved out of earshot of the butler whose duty was to accompany her that day.

'I knew it would happen sooner or later.' She said. 'Was he very stern about us seeing each other?'

'Very! I thought he was going to put a stop to us seeing each other but he just warned me politely not to get too fond of you Rosa, probably he thinks were too young to be serious about one another.'

'And what did you say to him then?'

'Oh I just said yes and no in what I thought were the right places, and when he quizzed me about my prospects I told him I was earning quite a lot of money, and hoped to do better in future.'
Rosa smiled at this. 'You must have said a few right things as he never mentioned anything to me this morning at breakfast but then perhaps he's saving it for later.'

'Perhaps no news is good news Rosa. Lets hope he does approve of us seeing each other, one thing does bother me though is just how long is he in this country for?'

Rosa thought for a moment before replying. 'At least another five years unless of course they decide to send him somewhere else but that's unlikely.'

Mikael looked slightly relieved at this and then decided to tell Rosa what he eventually intended to do about their relationship.

'Well Rosa I'm nineteen now and maybe next year if you'll agree we'll get engaged?'

Rosa smiled and although she'd half expected this she tried to look surprised.'Are you asking me to marry you then Mikael?'

'Of course. What else.'

'Aren't you supposed to go down on your knees for such a statement?'

'That's old fashioned and doesn't happen these days Rosa.'

'Maybe not. But a girl likes to think it does.'

Mikael paused a moment and glanced down at the slightly muddy grass, looked around ,then cautiously knelt beside Rosa.

'Well will you marry me Rosa?' He murmured.

'Of course I will. That's if my Parents agree but don't mention

Chapter Twenty Nine

Galina

Although life in Paris was quite satisfying for Galina she was by now missing her parents being so close by. Her business was quite enough to give her a good standard of living but she was still not satisfied and felt that life could be so much better. Many of her clients were English and spent a lot of their time travelling between London and Paris so she had contacts in London that would welcome her to be established there. Of course it would mean selling up most of her furniture if she decided to move to London but it would only take a few weeks to arrange and she had enough money in the bank to lease a good flat in the west end. She finally decided to move after giving it very careful thought in the spring of 1924 after receiving a written invite to Mikael's forthcoming marriage to Rosa. She hadn't seen him for almost six years but had heard from her parents of his good fortune and progress in the art world, now that he was marrying an ambassadors daughter this would really set him up for life.

After deciding on a definite move to London it only took a couple of visits to set up a flat near Park Lane and start the ball rolling with a few new clients and discreet adverts in the right places to earn her rent for the first few weeks. The prices that she charged were slightly higher than those for Paris but her clients were still keen to use her nevertheless, and she was very particular and fussy about taking on anyone that was not recommended. One of her first clients was a nearby hairdresser who passed on to her some of his very wealthy customers as did the local butcher, Galina returned the favour by doing the same for them and also giving them a discount.

It took a few weeks to build up the business to what she'd been used to in Paris by which time she'd managed to attract her local bank manager for a weekly visit. This was followed by a telephone call from a gentleman who had he said been recommended by the bank manager but wouldn't disclose his occupation. Galina didn't take long to discover that he was a bishop from out of town whose wife didn't seem to supply him with the usual services. So now she had a good cross section of the population ringing her bell in more ways than one. And with ample funds in the bank she could now think of taking a few days off to visit her family in the country. When calling on them she was more than surprised to find them living in such luxury compared to their dilapidated French farm and they were genuinely more than pleased to see her.

On showing her around the estate they seemed to be very much a part of the all round life there and appeared as though they'd lived there for years, they all seemed to speak English much better than she did. Galina resolved to book up for some special lessons when she got back to London as this might get her some more business. She spoke to her mother about Petra's marriage and asked if it would be suitable for her to call on her sometime, to which she said it was but not to mention to anyone just what she did for a living as it might spoil things for Petra.

'Whatever you do Galina don't let anyone in that house know what you are up to as they are very religious there and they don't even come across anyone in your line of business.'

She shook her head nervously. 'Of course not mother. I won't say anything I promise.'

Olga then decided to change the subject to avoid any further embarrassment. 'And how was life in Paris when you left Galina?'

'Very good mother but I was really missing you all and you seemed so far away living here. So I thought it would be nice to come and live here too.'

'And what's it like living in the middle of London Galina?'

'Very noisy at times but much the same as Paris and the food here is not so good is it?'

'You will get used to their ways Galina, but try and cook as much as possible yourself and it's cheaper. We have managed to arrange our food to be different with the cook here, she even likes eating our way now but the rest of the staff turn their noses up at the sight of it.'

'I don't get much time for cooking mother and anyway some of my customers insist on taking me out to eat in very nice places, so I just have to as they are, after all, paying for my services and they seem to enjoy doing it.'

Olga found it hard to understand why her lovely daughter was doing this for a living when she'd been brought up as a Christian and should have known right from wrong. But she had her own life to live and seemed happy enough in her own way, life never seemed to turn out as everyone expects.

'What does father say about me, is he angry mother?'

'Not really! He seems to accept it all just as long as you're happy Galina.'

When the time came to say goodbye Galina was close to tears and promised to come and visit them all at least once a month in future.

The children were thrilled that she'd taken the trouble to visit them especially as they hadn't seen her for such a long time, and long after she'd boarded the train on the journey home Anna was still very tearful thinking about that day's meeting.

Chapter Thirty

Another Wedding

Mikael found it a lot harder to come to terms with his courtship with Rosa than he'd ever imagined, this was despite attending various diplomatic functions with her and meeting very rich and important people. This was indeed a world apart from his one and he felt slightly uncomfortable about it all. His occasional meetings with his future father in law were a bit strained despite the fact that he was now agreeing to their getting married soon. His finances were much healthier now and good jobs were coming his way much more often, so much so that he had managed to rent a small flat near Regents Park owned by a relation of Rosa's father. Although he accepted this piece of good luck Mikael was suspicious that it was a cunning way of the family keeping an eye on Rosa.

The months leading up to the wedding day were hectic ones owing to the heavy workload and the furnishing of their new flat which seemed to keep Rosa happily involved. It was a large place with very ornate ceilings, not to Mikael's taste, but he would alter these once they had moved in, he just knew that the owner would be more than pleased with what he had in mind being a very religious person.

The fact that he was marrying the ambassadors daughter meant that the church service just had to be in the proper place and this part of the wedding was being looked after by Rosa's parents. It was as expected to be performed in Westminster Cathedral that being the most important and nearest church of their religion in the area. They also were paying for the reception at the Ritz Hotel afterwards and the honeymoon in Paris and Rome. All this part Mikael was slightly worried about as he'd so far led a quiet and ordinary sort of life but did feel happy about returning to Paris once again. This would be his chance to show off his knowledge of that city to Rosa and to visit his old college once again.

He felt that his mother approved of what he'd done with his life so far and had his father been still alive he would have as well, especially as he was marrying someone of the same faith. Perhaps somehow he was watching him from afar and guiding him in some way, he certainly hoped so. One thing that bothered him from time to time was the fact that each new job he started a very different picture came into his mind, it was as though there was someone or something actually guiding him each and every time. It was uncanny and very mysterious and in no way could he explain it he liked to think it was the fact that he'd attended the Leonardo School all those years ago, the tuition there had certainly left an impression on him. He also thought back to his weird experience whilst working on the ceiling at Charles's house that day was a turning point in his artistic life.

As the day of the wedding drew nearer Mikael started to have doubts about his marrying Rosa. It was not serious enough to say anything to her but it worried him especially when he lay awake some nights thinking about it. But this was a huge step he was taking and one not to be taken lightly and once done very hard to get out of, he sincerely hoped that Rosa was really in love with him as she said she was. The fact that they were going to live a reasonable distance from her parents was a slight consolation so perhaps they wouldn't interfere too much in their married life.

His mother helped pick his clothes for the wedding as he didn't know just what was needed and she was more than helpful having been at many society weddings during her years with Charles. She also took a keen interest in the way Rosa was choosing the furniture for the new flat without trying to appear too nosy, and this Rosa seemed to appreciate quite a lot. Petra not only helped guide her a little but also gave her tips on how to keep the costs down but at the same time buy quality things. Mikael couldn't avoid noticing how much his mother had changed in in the last few years she looked so much more sophisticated and sure of herself since her marriage to Charles. But her new position in life hadn't changed the way she still looked after them all and he hoped she was happy in her married life. It seemed like it the way she smiled most of the time.

When the day of the wedding came Mikael walked about in the house as though in a trance, he just couldn't believe it was all about to happen and his life was about to change dramatically. Suddenly he was no longer the son of a former chip shop owner but about to marry the daughter of an Ambassador, and it felt really strange so much so he had to pinch himself to believe it. It seemed like hours since he'd started to get ready and all the others were settled in their rooms waiting for the time to go by car to the church, he was really in no hurry to leave as everyone said the bride was always late arriving at the church.

This proved to be the case. So late was Rosa that Mikael wondered standing at the altar if she'd had second thoughts and changed her mind about the whole thing. He glanced at his watch nervously noting that she was by then fifteen minutes late and he sensed that others around him were also getting fidgety. His mother smiled nervously as if to reassure him that all was well and that it was the custom that they'd be kept waiting. Then suddenly the organist changed tune and Mikael breathed a sigh of relief his bride to be had at last arrived. Looking out of the corner of he eye he was aware of the splendour of the church and this was a situation he'd never expected to happen to him, and he felt so humble standing there waiting for one of the most important moments of his life.

The rest of the ceremony went without a hitch so did the reception although that part of the day was something Mikael could have done without, keeping a smile on his face was hard to do at times. He would have much sooner gone for a walk in the park with Rosa than pretend that he was enjoying himself. And just before midnight they both left the party to go home and change for their trip to Paris early the next morning,once alone in the back of the car they both felt at last free to talk about the days happening. This was to be the start of what they hoped to be a wonderful life together, and they were on their own free from all the restrictions that had been imposed upon them since they'd first started seeing each other. They hugged and kissed each other passionately in the darkness of the back of the car and couldn't wait to be completely alone later as man and wife. This was the time that they'd waited anxiously for for years now, neither of them now had any doubts that they'd done the right thing and nothing and nobody could ever come between them.

Chapter Thirty One

The Honeymoon

On their arrival at the George V Hotel on the Champs Elysėes Mikael was just slightly worried that this place was going to be a pain from the moment he saw the type of people staying there. But Rosa had herself been there many times before with her parents and it didn't bother her one bit to her it was a natural place to stay when in Paris. It turned out to be a bonus for them to be in the center and a short distance from most of the famous tourist spots plus quite some distance from the noisy traffic on the main road. Rosa made sure that Mikael always had enough coins in his pocket to tip the various staff as her father had taught her on previous visits. They spent quite a lot of time in their room and the staff must have been told that they were newly weds because they very rarely disturbed them.

Just as they were beginning to get used to the lazy style of living it was time to leave for Rome which when they arrived was so very busy and their hotel wasn't quite as smart as the one in Paris. It was however less than half a mile from Vatican City and slightly older than the last hotel. One week was only just enough to see most of the famous buildings and the amount of traffic and pace of life there was quite frightening. It was at times quite threatening to try and cross the busy roads and the difference in living quarters in various places was quite startling even more so than in London.

The time went even quicker than when in Paris as a lot of the more famous places took a long time to get to and they didn't want to miss any of it. Mikael didn't miss a thing during the visit to the Vatican and made numerous notes in the Sistine Chapel as cameras were not allowed inside there. But at the end of the week they were both a little weary and were glad of the thought of a rest on the train journey back home. It was whilst on the train that they began to discuss their travels since leaving England

and both came to the same conclusion. The first to bring up the subject was Mikael.

'Wouldn't it be a good idea if we both pooled our knowledge of another language to help each other Rosa.'

'In what way Mikael?' 'Well you teach me Italian' He said. 'And I'll teach you what French I know, obviously your knowledge is better, but I have always been able to get by alright in France.'

Rosa smiled and nodded. 'Of course why not. My French is only what I learned at school and isn't much use most of the time.'

'Good.' Replied Mikael. 'Now we can start just as soon as we get back home. This will be a great help for me when I need to speak to your relations sometimes. I feel a bit left out of things at times now.'
Speaking to each other was quite difficult with other passengers in the same carriage so they were pleased when night came and they moved to their sleeping carriage. It wasn't as restful though as the sound of the carriage wheels were a bit intrusive at times.

At Calais they boarded the ferry and the ship seemed to take forever to cross the channel due to the bad weather, Rosa spent the whole time on the bottom deck to avoid being tossed about too much. It was a relief for her to leave the boat and board the train for London, even the smell of the smoke from the engine made them both feel at home once more.

On arrival at their flat they decided to catch up on their sleep and not contact anyone for a few days, it took quite a while to sort their mail and read it all. One letter stood out from the rest it had an Italian stamp on it and Mikael couldn't resist opening it first before the others. To his dismay it was written in Italian so Rosa had to translate it for him and as she started Mikael began to realize that the writer wanted him to design and paint the ceiling in his Rome mansion. Mikael felt elated that his work was being recognized so far away as this but at the same time wondering whether he really wanted to travel so far to earn a living.

Rosa on the other hand was thrilled that her new husband should be offered such a job, she said she'd check with her father that the offer was a genuine one and the man would be able to pay for such an expensive project. She promised that if it turned out to be as good as it looked she would go with him to translate and assist in any way she could. The thought of them being apart saddened her after all they'd only been married a few weeks and so far life was good as it was. If Mikael agreed to do this their honeymoon would be extended and even living in a much cheaper hotel didn't bother her too much.

After the checks proved the job in Rome was really genuine and terms were agreed they left once again with the thought that it might be quite some time before their return. Rosa's father was more than impressed that his new son-in-law should be offered such an important project in Rome of all places, and at this rate Mikael would soon become one of the worlds leading mural artists.

Chapter Thirty Two

Living In Rome

Rome was very hot and buzzing with activity on the day they arrived and their main concern was to find the small hotel that they'd booked for a few weeks. It was nowhere near the standard of their previous one but it would have to do until they found out the true extent of the commission and whether it was going to be as profitable as they thought. The place was reasonably clean and the food good although a little less plentiful than they were used to, one consolation was that the staff were much fewer but much more friendly.

The following day they telephoned the house Mikael had agreed to work at and arranged to meet the owner Count Aldo Bortali at three o'clock. As they approached the huge mansion through the long drive two large Alsation dogs bounded towards them barking furiously. Fortunately the owner who had been watching soon had them under control and sent them away, Rosa white faced from the appearance of the dogs made their introductions and they went inside the house. On arrival in a large library the owner showed them to a seat. The Count, a tall thin good looking man, addressed them slowly in broken English.

'You have come to my attention through friends I have in England. They have seen some of your work there Mikael and assure me that you are are a very talented painter, so much so that I have brought you half way across the world to do something very special for me.'

Until now this house has been in my family for over two hundred years as a private residence but now I've decided to turn it into a very exclusive hotel. The first part of your contract will be to paint a large ceiling panel in the entrance hall which will include the family coat of arms, and afterwards one small painting in each of the twelve guest rooms all different of course.'

Mikael nodded. 'And would you like to suggest the theme of each one sir?'

'No just give me a rough sketch before you do them I will leave everything up to you just as long as they all have a Religious theme, that's all.'

Mikael looked satisfied at this. 'Can you show me please the location of the work area just so that I can make some notes of rough sizes and what they look like at present?'

'Of course! I'll show you now. Perhaps you'd like some coffee whilst you are looking?'

Mikael glanced at Rosa and she nodded. 'Thank you we would please.'

They were then taken back to the entrance hall and shown the position on the huge ceiling where the most important mural was to be situated. The Count then left them to arrange to have their coffee brought to them.

Mikael studied the ceiling for quite some minutes before writing some figures on his note pad by which time the servant had brought the very welcome coffee and cakes out to them. After sipping it Mikael had a really good look around noting the quality of the work overall. He then spoke quietly.

'This is a very grand place and deserves a really stunning piece of work on my part Rosa, and I shall take my time and fit something in that will hopefully impress him.'

At that point the Count returned and Mikael hurriedly finished his coffee before making a last minute request.

'Can I have a copy of your family coat of arms please just to make sure everything fits in together.'

The Count smiled and produced a bundle of papers from a nearby drawer. 'I thought that you'd ask for these and hope they will be of help to you.'

Mikael took the drawings and after glancing at them thanked him, he paused a moment thinking about his next move.

'I have a few things to shop for it might take a couple of days then I'd like to make a start on the work if possible?'

'That would be fine.' Replied the Count 'And I'll arrange the necessary ladders and platforms ready for you, is there anything else you need?' Mikael glanced up at the ceiling looking slightly worried.

'Would you like me to fill the whole ceiling area with my work ?'

'Yes of course.

'What about the chandelier in the middle then that is probably going to look out of place?'

'I'll get it removed then.' Said the Count.

Mikael nodded and looked satisfied with this answer. They then said goodbye and they left the building. It was only when they'd reached the main road that Rosa spoke, slightly relieved that the visit was over.

'Do you think that you can do something that will reach the standard of that fantastic workmanship in that entrance hall Mikael?'

Mikael grinned. 'Of course Rosa. This will be a simple task compared to some that I've done in London lately, there are so many examples all around here in Rome that I can't fail this time. And of course this will be a great selling point back home now that I've worked in Rome of all places. I can't wait to get started now so I'd better do a sketch of the first one for him to approve.'

Two days later he showed his rough sketches to the Count who beamed with satisfaction at the sight of them and Mikael inspected the scaffolding before starting his work. It took a whole week to sketch in the whole ceiling area to accommodate his work, and the family crest had to be modified slightly to blend in with rest of it.

It took over three months to complete the entrance hall ceiling before starting on the other smaller rooms elsewhere but the transformation was quite stunning, and the Count was more than pleased. So much so that he paid Mikael for the work to date and a bonus as well, plus he offered to accommodate them both in the first finished apartment free and their food to save the travel from the hotel each day.

Both Mikael and Rosa were well pleased and took his offer gladly especially as this would mean Rosa could relax in the apartment but be on hand to support him should he need it. It was during this time that she spent a lot of hours teaching him the basics of the Italian language, and Mikael certainly picked it up very quickly. Each of the apartments took about a week to complete and it was early winter when the whole thing was finished and they were looking forward to going home again to see their families and friends.

On the night before they left for home the Count gave a party in their honour and invited a few of his close friends to show off Mikael's fine work. Some of the very richest people in Rome were present and not only was it a showcase for the lavish apartments but a fantastic advert for Mikael's artistic work. At the party they were interviewed by the national press who also took countless photos of Mikael's ceiling.

It was later that night when alone in their room that Rosa broke the news that she was pregnant to Mikael, he was overjoyed at the prospect and knew that his mother would be as well.

When they arrived back home in London both their families had already been informed of their Roman adventure by the worlds press, mainly because one of the guests at their farewell party had been none other than Benito Mussolini who had been more than impressed by Mikael's work. Having just been elevated to the role of Prime Minister he had told a few people that he wanted to have Mikael do something similar for him. And the Italian Press had somehow picked up on this and the news had quickly got back to England, Rosa's father as Ambassador had been one of the first to hear of it. He warned Mikael not to be surprised to get an urgent call to return to Rome by the Prime Minister who usually got his way regardless of cost, Mikael was taken aback by this turn of events as he wasn't fully aware of the presence of the Prime Minister at the party. He had followed this man's progress through the past years and knew what a determined character he was so he rested awhile and awaited the outcome.

It wasn't long before he was summoned to the Italian Embassy and formally asked to meet the Prime Minister the following week at the Parliament Building in Rome, to discuss an important project. The tickets had already been arranged and paid for and the hotel in Rome booked as well, this was an offer he just couldn't refuse financially or otherwise. Mikael just couldn't believe his luck. This he felt sure was going to be the most important job he'd been asked to do so far. His only worry was that of meeting with Benito Mussolini and if half of what he'd read about him were true he was a hard man to deal with. He was also a little concerned that his Italian would be good enough to converse with a Prime Minister.

This was all unimportant to his mother compared to the fact that she would soon become a grandmother, something that made her very happy indeed.

Chapter Thirty Three

Benito Mussolini

The journey was quite pleasant and Mikael was treated like royalty with the added luxury of a chauffer driven Embassy car at Rome airport to take him to his hotel. The driver had instructions to collect him the following day to take him to the Parliament Building for the important meeting with the Prime Minister. Mikael had taken the trouble to read up on the life history of this very important man and was amazed to discover that his father was a blacksmith and mother a teacher. He was also a corporal in the Italian army in the 1914-18 war so he now knew that the man had very humble beginnings and this tallied a little with Mikael's peasant background.

The next day the car arrived as arranged and he was taken to the Parliament Building where armed guards were posted outside and looked very threatening, once inside the main building area the car stopped at the huge steps and a very smartly dressed man ran down to open the car door. He greeted Mikael and beckoned him to follow and once inside the huge doors took him down a long corridor to a large panelled office with several religious paintings on the walls. He was asked to wait whilst the Prime Minister was informed of his arrival, Mikael sat there in this rather strange silent room feeling a little apprehensive.

Suddenly the door to an inner office opened and a strange looking man walked in with a huge smile on his face he greeted Mikael like a long lost brother, and shook his hand warmly. This was completely out of character for the man as he always instructed his staff not to use the hand shake, under any circumstances.

'Hello Mikael. So glad you could come, sorry to drag you back to Rome so soon after your last visit but life here is very busy and we didn't catch you before you left for England.'

Mikael looked at him quizzically wondering just what sort of task was in store for him this time hoping that he'd be up to it. If the size of this place was anything to go by this man would be after something really special probably on the lines of the Sistine Chapel. The very thought of such an artistic project really frightened him, he smiled wondering how to answer but decided to just nod at this.

'After seeing your work at that party the other week I decided that we ought to have something like it for the general public to appreciate somewhere in the centre of Rome. So I asked my Minister of Art where would be the best place to have it, that is of course if you agree to do it for us?'

Mikael wondered what would happen to him if he refused and was an Italian citizen? The mind boggled so he decided that would be madness.

'Of course I will where did you have in mind?'

'Well I would have liked something in one our lovely churches but we are having a bit of trouble with His Holiness at the moment and he doesn't approve of much that I am doing, but he will do in time.'

Mikael wondered what his mother would have thought about all this.

'So where did you decide on then?'

Mussolini smiled. 'The church just outside the Vatican City boundary where they are planning to bury me when I die, that way I'll get away with it and the church can't object, can they?'

'No I suppose not Prime Minster, not if that's your final resting place.'

'I'm glad you agree. Now I will take you to this very splendid building and you can see for yourself the place we have chosen and when word gets out about this you'll find some very inquisitive Vatican officials watching your every move. They think that I'm a common upstart and shouldn't be Prime Minister.'

They left in the smart limousine tailed by a police escort and within minutes arrived at a huge building with guards outside everywhere.

Mussolini pointed to the building smiling 'This is a government building called the Palazzo Chigi and also a very famous tourist attraction. Nobody can stop me having something done in here, as I'm Prime Minister.'

Once out of the car and past the saluting guards they entered the building and walked slowly through the huge entrance hall full of ornate plasterwork and paintings. Here the Prime Minister paused a moment to explain what he had in mind.

'I will show you a place that is suitable but not one where Italian artists are prominent. We already have decided that you will one day soon be recognised as a unique artist, and this is going to be a feather in our cap to let you leave your mark here. And we just know you won't let us down.'

Mikael looked stunned at this statement and seemed lost for words for a second or two.

'Thank you for asking me Sir I only hope that I come up to your expectations. I must warn you that I'm not as good as Mikaelangelo, he was the worlds greatest and worked quite differently from me.'

The Prime Minister then carried on walking closely followed by Mikael to the rear of the entrance hall here he stopped and pointed to a large ornate ceiling area.

'Just here is where they are probably going to bury me one day so this part of the ceiling will be my present to the nation for the love they have given me over the past few years. So if this is favourable to you I will make the necessary arrangements for any help you want and passes to get in and out of here. They will also make an office available for your exclusive use Mikael. Now any questions please?'

'No not at the moment, you seem to have thought of everything.'

'Good! Just one thing we haven't finalised, that is your fee for this work. I will pay you personally on a basis of that what you got for your other job last time. Then nobody can say that I took it out of state funds, and the work will be recorded as being commissioned by myself. And one more thing I've arranged for a young artist from my home village to assist you and clean your brushes in exchange for a little tuition from you. His name is Mario and will be here just as soon as you want to start.'

'That will be a big help and I could start in two days time that will give your people time to do the platform, and for me to get some paints, if that's enough time for you Sir?'

The Prime Minister looked pleased at this.'That can be arranged very quickly. I'll do it now as soon as you leave and I'm sure this will be a successful venture for us both Mikael.'

He shook hands and Mikael turned to leave happy in the knowledge that this would turn out as good if not better than anything he'd done previously.

On the day that Mikael commenced work at the Palazzo sure enough everything was ready for him and the young artist Mario was there to welcome him with a smiling face. The first thing he arranged was coffee and biscuits for them both and they sat in the office drinking it whilst Mario awaited eagerly his instructions.

'Well Mario I hope you will learn something from the way I go about this painting and you will soon see how important the planning is before starting such a job.'

The boy looked at him as he put on his old clothes ready to make a start and picked up a pencil, ruler, and sketches then beckoned Mario to follow him from the office and up the ladder to the corner of the ceiling.

'Now the first thing to do is measure the distance of the four corners of the area to be painted to note what this all is, then roughly sketch each part in so it all looks balanced.'

Mario nodded and although he'd got the general picture of what Mikael was saying his knowledge of English wasn't all that great.

This was obvious to Mikael so he thought he'd make something very plain from the start.

'The first and hardest part of this job is painting something above your head.' He raised his arm with the elbow resting on the scaffold board to demonstrate.

'When you've done this for a few hours your arm will really ache like never before, and at the end of the first day it will hurt unless you have exercised it a lot beforehand.'

Mikael then started to measure the ceiling a bit at a time then placed a series of dots in various parts after checking his sketches. It was quite some hours before he looked satisfied and put down his things and he motioned Mario to follow him back to the office. There they had some lunch and afterwards took the paints and brushes back to the scaffold and Mikael started his painting.

By the finish of the first week the work was starting to look quite good and Mikael seemed reasonably pleased with it, he was also, with careful questioning, able to gain some information about the Prime Minister. It seemed that a large section of the working class were behind him and liked his ideas regarding drastic changes in the way the country was being run, and unemployment was slowly going down. So this was quite contrary to what the British press were saying and that he was a warmonger and taking the country down the wrong path.

The following weeks passed very quickly and it was noticeable how many curious people appeared every so often and stared at the work. The Prime Minister came at least once a week and seemed to find no fault at all in it, on one visit he was accompanied by the Minister of Art who praised the work himself. On the completion the Prime Minister paid him in person and said that it was the best piece of modern religious painting he'd ever seen. He also said that he'd arrange that if Mikael wanted to visit Italy again he would be treated as a V.I.P. Little did Mikael know how this man was to become the overall ruler within a few short years of that country. One of the shrewd moves by Mussolini was his conversion from Atheism to the Roman Catholic faith and this seemed to please the Pope and helped slightly to heal the rift that had come between them.

Mikael was soon on his way home and although quite a lot richer and pleased with his task he was anxious to get home to his new wife and family. He was just weeks away from the birth of his child and Rosa was so relieved to see him home before this happy event.

Chapter Thirty Four

The First Child

Back at home the word had already got out that Mikael had accomplished something no British artist had done for centuries, completing an artistic work in a public building in Rome. It was then that offers of work started to come thick and fast and Mikael had a job to sort out the best of them. There were quite a few from around the north London area so he whittled them down with the help of Rosa to just three and negotiated a fair price on each.

It was just as he was half way through the first painting that Rosa's father the Ambassador was informed that he was needed in Paris as their man was about to retire. This was a blow to Rosa who had never been far away from her family before and Mikael was reluctant to leave his work at this stage, there was too much at stake. He had long discussions with Rosa and his mother regarding this turn of events and decided against any thought of moving to France in the near future. This was to prove the right decision for him because some of the very large projects he was given over the next few years enabled him to amass large sums in the bank. He was becoming a reasonably rich young man but to all those who knew him well still a very likeable and quietly unassuming person.

It came as a shock when a very rich Embassy asked him to transform a room ceiling for them in the fresco style, something that he'd never attempted before. Although he'd read numerous articles on this type of work he didn't feel capable of doing such a thing especially in such a prominent place. He did however manage to put them off by saying he was busy for the next two years, but would think about it. He then spent many months planning to practise on one of the ceilings in his own house to see if it worked out. This became a trial and error exercise that involved removing unwanted plaster from the already ornate cornices of the ceiling, then after numerous frustrating attempts he at last managed to conquer the very skilled job. He knew it was going to be very difficult because it took Michaelangelo many years to complete just the first half of the Sistine Chapel, he was after all the master of this craft and had the help of a few other artists. The finished job looked very professional but Mikael decided at this point to give up any attempt to offer his services on such a piece of delicate artistic work again, better to stick to what he knew best.

It was during this that something happened to disturb him one late afternoon the quiet atmosphere was broken by what seemed like a very familiar soft voice behind him saying the plaster was too soft and to wait a minute. He looked around but there was nobody there then it dawned on him he'd heard that same voice in Charles's house all those years ago whilst painting his ceiling. He felt very strange afterwards but when he viewed the section he'd been working on at the time the whole piece looked much brighter than the rest. Maybe there was someone up there guiding him after all.

His work was interrupted for a few days when Rosa gave birth to a very beautiful baby girl they named Rosanna. This child was to grow up with all the best characteristics of her father and become a very determined and resourceful human being.

Chapter Thirty Five

Petra

Marriage on the whole had made Petra slightly happier than she had imagined it would despite the fact that she still couldn't come to terms with sleeping with Charles. Financially she was so much better off than she'd ever been in her life before and her children seemed happy enough and had long ago come to terms with having a step-father. Charles thought the world of them and was very proud to call them his children. He still seemed to work very long hours at the bank and Petra kept on urging to take things a little easier and spend more time at home. His house in the country was doing exceptionally well with rising attendances by the public each year bringing in almost enough to offset the running of the place.

Olga and Yuri were really happy in their small cottage and said it was heaven working with so many happy people, they were forever thanking Petra for finding them such a well paid job in England.

Their two children both with good jobs and prospects spent a lot of their spare time helping their parents and taking them out for car rides Petra's Anna was now in charge of the export department where she worked which had grown enormously since her arrival there. Nica who'd started in a dress shop was now a very fashionable designer in the West End. And Boris the youngest son was a qualified architect working for a large building company. So all in all Petra was quite satisfied the way things had turned out for all of them. She often wondered how life would have turned out had their been no war all those years ago, she'd still swap her present life for the one with Ivan and missed him still. But there was no turning the clock back now she just had to make the best of what she'd got. So now she was on her own for the first time with all her children living in their own places and life slightly emptier than it had been for years.

The house was very easy to run with so many servants to keep the place clean although she still done a lot of it herself to fill in the day when not out shopping. It was a huge place for just two of them but Charles said that he needed it for entertaining his very rich friends and clients. Petra looked at the huge bills from the stores for food sometimes and thought back to how much she'd spent at the fish shop in the Old Kent Road. What they used now would have almost fed the whole street back then, and she felt sad at the thought of all those hungry children who eagerly awaited closing time at the shop for the left-overs of the fish crackling. She hoped they were better off now and that their parents had a little more money to feed them.

Chapter Thirty Six

1936

The next few years were good ones for the family and Mikael and Rosa were by now able to buy outright a fairly large house in Hampstead with enough extra rooms to have a nursery in it. Their baby Rosanna was by this time three years old and growing fast It was early spring when a well dressed man called asking to speak to Mikael about some business. Rosa was a bit suspicious and asked him to call back that evening when Mikael would be home. This he agreed to and left his card, he said it was about a possible trip abroad. The name on the card was of a Captain Andrew Philips what that meant to Rosa was a bit of a puzzle as she'd never heard Mikael speak of him.

Later that evening the same man came back and Mikael answered the door to him and they went into the living room to talk.

This was the first time that Mikael had set eyes on the man and he was very curious to know what he had to say.

'My name is Captain Andrew Philips and I work for the Ministry of Arts and Education. Sorry to disturb you at such a late hour but something important has happened and we thought that you may be able to help us in a little matter.'

Mikael looked a bit puzzled what could the Ministry want with him.

'How can I help you?

The man shifted nervously. 'Well it's come to our notice that you where at some stage quite friendly with Benito Mussolini. Is that not so?'

Mikael looked suspiciously at the man. The Dictator as he was now known didn't have a good reputation in the western world.

'Yes I did a painting for him a few years ago.'

The man smiled. 'Yes we know that and he has always regarded you as a most helpful artist and we wondered if you'd like a trip to Rome with a delegation of Ministry Personnel to pave the way with Mussolini who is the overall head of their Ministry of Culture.

'In what capacity?'

'We would give you a top artistic rank and a very good fee if you accept our offer.'

'And what would the object be of all this?'

The man coughed nervously. 'We would like you to try and gain Mussolini's confidence a little, and also learn a bit of what the man in the street thinks about the way their country is being run.

'What leads you to think that I'd be up to the job then?'

The man took a sheaf of papers from his coat pocket.

'We have checked on your credentials so you pass for one of the most honest citizens in this country and are a most intelligent man, we know almost everything about you.'

Mikael looked bewildered at all this.

'But I have no training in such things or experience in diplomatic affairs.'

'Don't worry about that we will give you a few days lessons in London before you go, that's of course if you agree to go?'

'Supposing I refuse. ' Said Mikael. 'What then?'

'That's your decision. But if you do you must never mention what I've told you today. '

'What about my Italian speech then it's not all that good?'

'It seems to have got you by last time you were there.'

'Ah but my wife who is Italian was with me then.'

'She can go with you, all expenses paid, if you like. We have got one interpreter going already, but it would be nice to have another'

At this Mikael looked more interested.

'Now this sounds like a good job. When is it likely to happen?'

'In two weeks time so we'll need your answer very soon. And there is a possibility that we may have a future job for you as an interpreter because of your language skills, and that will be very highly paid.'

'This is a bit unexpected. Can I call you about my answer I have to speak to my wife first?'

'Yes of course. Here's my telephone number. I do hope you decide to go it will be a good experience for you.'

The man then shook hands and left, Mikael stood watching him walk away down the drive and it took quite some time to recover from what he'd been told. He then walked back into the kitchen to tell the news to Rosa who stood anxiously waiting to know what it was all about. He knew that there were parts that he couldn't tell her and that was going to be difficult.

Rosa was the first to speak. 'What was all that about then?' She said.

'He's asked me to go to Rome.'

'To do some painting?'

'No just to attend an artistic conference there, and you can also come as well.'

'What's brought this up then?'

'It seems that Mussolini has asked that I attend and they probably don't want to offend him. So they are going to pay me to do it, that's if we agree.'

Rosa looked at him curiously. 'And do you want to?'

'I said I'd think about it. That's all.'

'How long is it for. Did he say?'

'It's not certain yet, maybe a week.'

'Then I think we should say yes. This will give you a little break from painting and who knows what future opportunities it might open for you Mikael.'

He looked at Rosa in surprise not expecting such a positive and quick answer. 'I will call the man first thing in the morning then and say we'll go then Rosa.'

The next day Mikael called Captain Philips to confirm that they were both willing to go to Rome and he made an appointment for them to attend a short briefing the following week in Whitehall in his office. His instructions were simple just to bring the passports to check that they were in order and to give them Diplomatic Immunity for the trip. He also said he'd give instructions at the entrance of the Foreign Office to let them in by showing their passports and giving his name.

On their arrival at the appointed time and date both Mikael and Rosa were a bit taken aback at the size of the building they were going to be interviewed in. The guard on the door once they identified themselves smiled and called for an escort to take them to the right office. There they were asked to wait in a huge outer room overlooking the Mall and Buckingham Palace they were the only ones seated there and both felt like V.I.P.s. After only a matter of minutes a tall very smart man in his fifties came out from an inner office to greet them. 'So sorry to keep you both waiting. Won't you please come inside.'

They followed him into a slightly smaller office where he indicated two seats in front of a very large mahogany desk which he then sat behind.

'First of all my name is Colonel James Faversham and I've been asked to brief you both about your forthcoming trip to Rome for us. What we didn't realize was that you madam were our last Italian Ambassador's daughter, and maybe know as much about Diplomatic Protocol as we do, and for this I do apologise most sincerely.'

Rosa smiled. 'Don't worry I haven't had much experience of meeting heads of state yet not even my own. Benito Mussolini was only Prime Minster when we last met him.'

'That is what I need to talk to you mainly about.' Said the Colonel.

'At this time we are a little hesitant about sending large groups of people to Italy for political reasons that's why we have selected you.'

'You mean it's dangerous out there?' Said Mikael.'

'Not really but there are all sorts of rumours coming out that Italy has occupied Ethiopia and they are about to decide on whether to throw in their lot with Adolph Hitler. So far though it's still safe to travel there for short periods and you will be safe enough for your mission.'

'What exactly do you want me to do there Sir?'

'Not much really just keep your ear to the ground and smooth the way for the others you're going with. This may be the last chance we have should war break out of contact with Mussolini.'

'And what about the other members of the party. What is their mission?'

'They will be an odd bunch but some will be high ranking diplomats trying to get some assurances from whatever source as to the Italian position should Hitler push into another country.'

Rosa looked slightly worried. 'Do you think that they may occupy France then, my father is ambassador in Paris?'

'Possibly. But we will get quite an early warning should that happen. This of course could be months rather than weeks away so it won't affect you, and your father will get to know about any problems before most people.'

'What if we are threatened in any way . What then?'

'We have a very efficient Embassy there and the staff will be monitoring your movements. And anyway Adolph Hitler will have his hands full for a few months with the Olympic Games and the eyes of the world will be on him.'

'When we speak to Mussolini just how do we address him?'

'Now that's a tricky one because he's a dictator. Just leave it to our diplomats to speak first but in your case I'd call him Sir that's all. He'll probably treat you like a long lost friend from what we've heard.'

Mikael smiled at this. 'So nice to be so popular.'

The Colonel nodded. 'You'd be amazed how much you are especially now that your work is included in the Tourist Travel lists in Rome. And you have to queue for hours to get in to see it.'

'And when do you need us to leave then Sir?'

'A week today but we'll telephone you soon to confirm the time and where to pick up the tickets at the airport. If there are any changes beforehand we will let you know.'

The Colonel then rose and made to end the meeting and shook hands with them both. 'So glad to have had the pleasure of meeting you both and I'm sure you will have a pleasant time in Rome it's not too hot there yet this early in the year.'

Chapter Thirty Seven

Back to Rome

At Croydon Airport the following week the tickets were at the reception and already the party travelling with them were already gathered, including the senior diplomat in charge of them. They were as expected a truly mixed bunch of all ages and characters ten men and two ladies including Rosa, but they looked a reasonably happy crew. They introduced themselves and then prepared to depart on the journey, this was pleasant as they were booked in as government officials and first class V.I.Ps and there were no customs involved.

On arrival at their hotel in Rome they were warmly greeted by the manager, and then shown their rooms, which were all very luxurious, and well ventilated, despite the very hot weather outside. At dinner that evening they were told by the senior diplomat that there would be a formal meeting the next morning to discuss their mission and allocate the different tasks. This would be held in a very private office in the hotel. Mikael hoped that nothing would be mentioned that Rosa didn't know about already he feared that there might be a conflict of interests, that she might want to tell her father about. This might of course not be the case as Mussolini could possibly want to see him regarding something completely different.

The following morning after breakfast they all assembled in the private well decorated conference room waiting for the senior diplomat to make an appearance. Before he appeared Mikael and Rosa tried to find out what some of the others knew about the mission, but some seemed very secretive indeed. When the man in charge Major Thomas finally appeared grim faced they sat there wondering what could have happened overnight that could have gone wrong. They were however soon to find out when he began to address them in a slow serious tone of voice.

'Ladies and Gentlemen I'd better start by telling you first of all why we are here, and it's probably slightly different from what you've been led to believe already. The plan originally was two-fold, the first part was political and half of us are here to monitor if possible the Italian Government's real future intentions in Spain regarding the civil war there. The second objective is a cultural and artistic exchange of views which is being overseen by Benito Mussolini himself, and initially he was keen to spend as much time on it as possible. However something has come up that may alter our plans somewhat and we may have to shorten our trip by a day or so. Unfortunately last night Italy invaded the island of Majorca and there is a little problem over this although our government has shown signs of approval so far, things could possibly change. There is also a small problem with Ethiopia as well but that's another story. So therefore from this afternoon we shall split into two groups, the political section, the other one cultural and artistic headed by Mikael here and his good lady wife Rosa.' He points to them both.

'The first meetings will be held here in this hotel and your welcoming Italian delegates will be in the selected rooms on the list I shall give you.' He then passed them each a list with the times and venues typed on them and waited whilst they glanced at the contents.

'Now as you can see Benito Mussolini who likes to be addressed as Il Duce is not present for this afternoon's sessions, but promises to attend both section meetings tomorrow hopefully. Now are there any questions at this point?'

There was a silence as they glanced around at each other before Mikael spoke. 'I see on the list that we are going to be shown around most of the historic sites of Rome and I'm assuming some of us have spent quite a lot of time here already in the past, don't you think that a waste of time? Major Thomas nodded. 'I thought someone might bring that up and quite rightly so, the answer is just grin and bear it, try and be as friendly as possible we might hopefully come away from here with some of the right answers to take back home with us.'

This proved to be a very sensible comment the following day when Il Duce started his talk with the artistic group, and Mikael was slightly embarrassed when what looked like his work was singled out to be the first on the guided tour by Mussolini himself.

As he assembled them in the Pallazo Chigi Parliament building he let them study the ceiling for a few minutes before speaking.

'Tell me do any of you know, apart from the artist himself just who did this wonderful work?'

They all looked slightly puzzled as it was not as yet listed in many English travel books. Only one person apart from himself knew the answer and Mikael stayed silent, Mussolini smiled and went on to tell them it was Mikael their leader. His next question was a little more puzzling.

'Look very carefully and see if you can fault it in any way?'

They all looked up again and were silent for quite some time only one of the group seemed to feel he knew the answer that Mussolini was maybe looking for. He raised his hand nervously.

'Could the answer be that it would have been done better in the fresco style Sir, like Michaelangelo's work?'

Mussolini's face lit up. 'You are right first time and many prominent artists from around the world have said the same thing about it, but I personally like it very much and do not want it altered in any way. So Mikael I will speak to you again in private about doing another ceiling for me somewhere else in this very beautiful building.'

They all looked at Mikael realizing at this point just why he'd been chosen as their leader.

Mussolini glanced at his watch thoughtfully. 'Unfortunately I have another appointment very soon so I will leave you in the capable hands of our Minister of art Signor Victor Beretta who will be here in a moment to take you on a short tour of our most important buildings. And another one of my ministers has arranged a special private viewing of the Sistine Chapel for you all, I personally couldn't get involved in this as His Holiness the Pope and I disagree on a few small matters at the moment.'

He then left the room and the art Minister appeared minutes later to escort them around a few famous buildings within the centre of the capital, most of these Mikael had already seen on previous visits but he had a little more time to examine the paintings at his leisure on this occasion. This was the first time that the group began to talk openly about the reason they'd been chosen for the trip, and it was interesting for Mikael and Rosa to discover that, apart from Robert Field who was a sculptor, the others were either musicians or actors. They all seemed to be in awe of Mikael having seen his painting and then having it explained in great detail by Mussolini earlier in the day.

Later whilst alone in their hotel room Rosa started to question Mikael about the what he knew about their invitation to Rome.

'Do you really think Mussolini wants you to paint another ceiling Mikael?'

He looked at her and smiled with satisfaction. 'Yes I think so. He's a man who usually gets what he wants, but he seems to have his hands full at the moment.'

'You mean the war in Ethiopia?' Replied Rosa.'

'Yes and with Majorca as well he'll be too busy to worry about my painting a ceiling for him.' He paused a moment before continuing. 'There is something that I have to tell you in strict confidence and so please don't tell your father this. As a favour for the Foreign Office I promised to speak to a few ordinary locals in Rome about their opinion of Mussolini as a ruler, so when we get a few hours to spare perhaps you could help me?'

Rosa looked at him for a moment. 'Why you.? What's wrong with the diplomats doing this?'

'They thought I'd get a better answer than they would Rosa, don't you think?'

'Maybe. But we'd have to ask a few in the poorer parts.'

Mikael was relieved to have got over the problem of explaining his part of the deal with the Foreign Office, and hoped that the answers he got were going to satisfy them.

Two days later they did get the chance to quiz quite a few people and were slightly surprised at the answers they received. It seemed that the majority were in favour of Mussolini as he'd lowered unemployment drastically by spending huge amounts on new roads and tunnels through the mountains. What they didn't realize was that he was spending further large amounts on his ambitious war programmes especially the Spanish civil war. He was also a very feared man with secret police openly taking away and killing those in opposition to his policies. His love of artistic monuments and art in general was well known and he was now approving spending on large projects in the Rome area. This was his way of showing the public that he was a cultured man by leaving something they'd hopefully remember him by.

The following day there was news from London that they must all return for their safety, Mikael and Rosa were instructed to visit Mussolini at the Ministry where they hoped to get some news from him regarding the job he'd promised Mikael. Unfortunately he was unable to see them but sent a note to wish them well and safe journey home. He also said he'd contact Mikael very soon when things settled down. Unfortunately this never happened as Italy got bogged down in fighting for the next few

Chapter Thirty Eight

A new assignment

On arrival back in London Mikael was asked quietly by the leading diplomat to attend a briefing the next day at the Foreign Office to discuss the trip in detail, also they wanted to pay him his fee. This made Mikael feel slightly nervous wondering what if anything they would make of his findings or were they setting him up for something else. Together with Rosa they said their goodbye's to the others and left on the train for home.

At the appointed time Mikael arrived at the Foreign Office where he was shown into the same office as before, but this time he faced not only the man who'd interviewed him previously but also another very serious looking middle aged man. They both shook his hand and the other man introduced himself.

'Thank you Mr Garodny for being so punctual. My name is Lord James Carlyle and I believe you've already met my colleague Captain Philips here?'

Mikael nodded. 'Yes we met here some weeks ago.'

Lord Carlyle then moved a chair in front of the desk and sat facing Mikael looking slightly more relaxed. Captain Philips picked up a file from the desk and took out a cheque from it this he passed to Mikael smiling. I hope you and your wife had a pleasant journey and this will compensate you both for your efforts.'

Mikael glanced at the cheque and was very surprised at the amount, it was more than he'd ever been paid for painting ceilings.'

'Thank you this is more than I expected and I hope the mission was a success even though it was shorter than planned?'

Lord Carlyle then took up the conversation. 'Yes it went quite well considering the problems our people had with Mussolini. Now then what first of all did you make of your encounter with him, was he as friendly as you previously found him on your last trip?'

Mikael thought for a moment. 'Yes he was. And he seemed genuinely pleased to see me again, and spoke about offering me another job in the Ministry in Rome.'

'And do you think he meant it?'

'Well he gave me that impression.' Mikael then took a folded report from his pocket and handed it to Lord Carlyle who then read it carefully before speaking again.

'This is very well written and interesting, you seem to have done a good job talking to quite a few people in Rome Mr Garodny. Our people should be very impressed with you for this information. Now I'd like to make you an offer but what I have to say must be in strict confidence whether you accept it or not.'

Mikael looked at him a moment. 'What is it you want me to do then?'

Lord Carlyle picked up a file from the desk. 'It says here that you speak Russian fluently and several other languages including French, is that not so?'

Mikael nodded. 'Yes I do.'

'Excellent! Well then this is what we propose to offer you and it's on a long term contract, maybe for a number of years certainly no less than five. Our offer is the salary of a Captain in the British army and all that goes with it for your part time services as an interpreter.

Now you may only be used for two months at a time for now but should war break out it will be a full time job, if that happens we will increase your salary quite substantially. Does this appeal to you?'

Mikael looked a bit puzzled at this offer and sat there some seconds before replying. 'What exactly will be my duties be sir?'

'Well not much really but we will have to acquaint you with people working for us at certain listening radio stations occasionally just to make sure you keep in touch with the way we do things in our department.'

'Does this mean some sort of intelligence work then?'

'Just checking translation!' Lord Carlyle replied. 'But you won't be a spy as such just checking on things for us in a professional way.'

'And what if I turn down your offer?

'We are not in any way trying to blackmail or frighten you but should there be a war in the immediate future there are a few options to consider. The first is that you hold a Russian passport and that may not be in your interest, secondly your wife has an Italian one and she could be interned should Mussolini link up with the Germans against us.'

Mikael looked uneasy. 'And how will you get over that should war happen and I accept?'

Lord Carlyle smiled. 'Simple really! We will issue you both with British passports.'

'In that case I accept your offer in the hope that I can explain some of this to my wife.'

'Good that's wise of you! Now I'll let Captain Philips fill you in on the details of your work. And by the way you can carry on painting during the time that you are not engaged in our work.'

Mikael thanked him and the spent the next hour being briefed by Captain Philips in another office. He left the building slightly bewildered as to just why they'd chosen him of all people. Thinking over the terms of what he'd been offered everything looked very favourable indeed, and even the thought of being caught up in a war still didn't worry him unduly. It would be better than being called up to fight. On his way home he carefully planned just what he would tell Rosa and what to leave unsaid so as to not worry her about his future, after all he was in no way being groomed as a spy, or was he?

Chapter Thirty Nine

Station X

The next few months were busy ones for Mikael because in between his painting jobs he spent time travelling to far away Government radio listening posts, assisting translating various messages from all parts of Europe. It was during these visits that he discovered that there were many more just like him doing the same thing, this made him think that there was more to this task he'd been given to understand.

It was late October in 1937 when he was instructed to pay a short visit to a secret place they named Station X, he realised he was now a trusted top line translator, and that all the other posts were sending messages to this place. What happened next left him in no doubt that the British Government were actually preparing for war. His training was suddenly increased and they seemed to be preparing him for bigger things. Without any confirmation his usual monthly salary cheque doubled so he then felt things were about to change dramatically. His main tasks included mostly Russian and a small amount of German messages, so he now felt certain that the Germans were getting ready to occupy adjoining lands.

He seemed to have assured Rosa that the new job was a reasonably safe one, despite her knowing almost all that was going on in Italy through her father in Paris. So far he not been away from home for more than two days at a time but this was about to change during the coming months. It was at Station X that he saw at first hand the preparations that were going on there to accommodate a small army of people and machinery for something big. He was told not to speak to anyone about what was happening in the complex and that he'd only be there a few weeks at the most, as others were going to replace him on a permanent basis.

In the grounds of the estate was a very imposing large manor house that had been taken over by the ministry quite recently, this was being used as a headquarters for top officials. Back from the road and out of sight to the public military sentries stood guard night and day, and nobody was allowed in without a pass.

On the last few days of his stay he noticed more and more both men and women arriving at the complex and he was struck by the fact that they were either very rich or extremely well educated. They certainly wouldn't be from the Old Kent Road. Their hands showed no sign of manual work, and they all spoke in a most peculiar way, trying hard not to open their mouths too much. It was as though they'd all gone to the same university and been taught to speak that way.

Although the staff took their meals in a large dining hall in the main house most of the staff including Mikael were billeted in guest houses in the nearby towns and villages. The owners of these had obviously been well vetted by the ministry beforehand as they never asked awkward questions about their tenant's occupations.

At the end of this task he was instructed to go home and rest until January when he would start training for a new part of his job, the instructions for this would be confirmed during the following month. He felt that things were about to change owing to the huge increase in salary, they wouldn't be paying him that much for doing such simple translating.

It was a relief when it was time to leave this cold damp place and return to his nice warm house in London and be with Rosa for Christmas hopefully. This was to be his last rest period for quite some time as events in Europe took a turn for the worse from then on, and Mikael was to be kept very busy indeed in a way he didn't expect.

Chapter Forty

Basic Training

After returning home Mikael spent a blissful Christmas period together with short visits to both their families, but before they went he briefed Rosa about saying nothing about his new job. If questions were asked he was still only a ceiling painter and an antique dealer with plenty of work all the time. The visit to Paris was a little more tricky as her father was slightly more difficult to talk to as his country Italy was then wavering on the decision by Mussolini whether to join the German dictator Adolph Hitler in his fight against democracy. He was a bit tight lipped as to his views on the way Italy was now being run and what he believed in might just cost him his job ultimately.

It was late January when Mikael finally received his instructions to report for basic training at the military training camp at Sandhurst. This was organised in a special area for making sure that prospective officers would become basically fit for certain overseas duties. He was advised to say nothing about his rank of Captain or his salary to anyone, and he would pass out as the others would at the end of the course.

After kitting out with uniforms they were shown their huts by very serious drill instructors who pointed out the way the way the huts should be kept. This was a rude awakening for most of them as they'd mainly had a very sheltered upbringing. They were treated with some respect for most of their stay but many of the lower rank instructors were a bit brutal at times. Mikael felt he was reasonably fit compared to most of the others but within weeks they all showed a great improvement.

When the passing out day came there were only two failures who were both sent home as unfit in the last week. Mikael had the highest marks in most disciplines in his section but still hoped that war could be averted.

On arrival back in London the first thing that caught his eye was the newspaper placard outside the station saying Anthony Eden resigns as Foreign Secretary. He bought a paper and glanced at the details it seemed that Eden was against the policy of appeasement with Mussolini by Neville Chamberlain, this didn't make much sense to Mikael as he'd lost contact with world news in camp. He hurried on home by taxi hoping life would be as normal there as when he'd departed.

His arrival back home in Hampstead brought Rosa smiling to the door she hugged him as he dropped his kit in the hallway, then stood back smiling.'My you do look well Mikael! But your face is so thin have they been starving you?'

He shook his head smiling. 'No far from it, they fed us well most of the time.'

She looked at his kitbag and studied it carefully.

'Does it mean you are in the army now then?'

Mikael paused before answering. 'Not really! I only have to wear the uniform should war break out. Please don't ask too many questions that I can't answer.'

He took off his coat and walked into the kitchen. 'I'd love a cup of tea before you tell me all the news that's happened whilst I've been away.'

Rosa moved away to put the kettle on then got the cups from the cupboard.

'Your mother called last week and wants you to telephone her, she said that Charles has a few problems at work.'

'O.k. I'll call her tomorrow. But what have you been up to?'

'Not much really. Just shopping and visiting friends that's all.'

'What about you, did you get on alright?'

Mikael nodded. 'Yes it was much better than I thought it would be.'

Rosa poured out the tea she was making and placed it on the kitchen table. They both sat down and looked at each other for quite some time without speaking. Mikael had missed her badly whilst he'd been away.

They drunk the tea quickly and still without a word got up and walked hand in hand silently upstairs to the bedroom. They hadn't felt quite like this since the first days of their married life and being apart for just a few weeks seemed like a lifetime.

Chapter Forty One

The Second World War

It was the next day when Mikael remembered to call his mother so after breakfast he rang her. She was more than relieved to hear his voice and sounded very worried, then after enquiring about his trip then told him the bad news.

'It's Charles that I want to tell you about.' She said. 'His bank is in money trouble the stock market crashed last week, and he's lost most of his money. And that means he will have to sell his country house for what he can get for it.'

Mikael looked worried at this news and it was quite some seconds before he answered.

'And what about the house that you are living in mother?'

'Oh that's alright! I've just told him to get rid of all the servants that's all, we can manage without them quite easily.'

There was a silence before Michael spoke again.

'What about Yuri and Olga then mother, what will they do now?'

'That's not a problem Mikael. Yuri has been promised a share in a farm back in France by a friend whose father died and left him it in his will. And providing they do their share of the work on it they should be alright. The only trouble is the friend doesn't know anything about farming.'

'That sounds a bit risky mother are they sure about this?'

'They seem to be.' Replied Petra. 'I hope it works out for them but anyway they can always come back and stay with us if it doesn't.'

'And what does Charles say about that?'

'He says it's alright for them to live here if anything goes wrong with the French farm and I'm sure he means it, he's a very generous man deep down.'

'He must be mother to suggest such a thing if he's got serious money problems himself. If there's anything I can do let me know obviously you and Charles are in a different world to me as regards money, but you can call me if you need some.'

'Thank you Mikael but we can manage, that is if Charles can get rid of the country house soon.'

Before Mikael could answer the letterbox rattled and a bulky envelope landed on the floor near his feet, he bent down to pick it up.

'Sorry mother that was the mail. It looks very important I'll call you back later.'

He replaced the receiver and went into the living room to read the letter. It was from the Foreign Office and wanted him to report there in a weeks time for instructions, he then feared the worst that war was imminent.

His first instinct was to tell Rosa but to reveal maybe the full extent of his role in anything should he be needed was risky, as she and all Italian subjects living in England might eventually be interned should Italy join forces with Germany. This was one question he needed to ask about most urgently, and her going to France to join her father looked very dangerous as the Germans would almost certainly occupy it soon.

His trip to the Foreign Office turned out to be more interesting than he expected because not only were the usual officials present but a portly important looking man there who they introduced as Winston Churchill. He was there to sit in on Mikael's interview and pass comment. This was the first time they'd met and Michael was slightly nervous knowing the man's reputation. Churchill's interest in this interview soon became apparent, he was then trying to form an alliance with France and Russia against the German government. He was also interested in this formation of an Alpine post bordering on the Italian frontier. This was to be the start of what later became known as Churchill's secret army.

Colonel Faversham was the first to start the meeting with the others all seated around an oval office table.

'First of all Mikael what you are about to hear this afternoon must never be repeated to anyone, do you understand?'

Mikael nodded. Of course.'

'Good! Now we are about to put together a group of experts to work as a team in the French Alps in case troops from any friendly nations need assistance now that the Germans are attacking neighbouring countries. Your role together with others is to make sure they reach safety and you will all be trained in various skills to do this. We realise it will be cold and dangerous in the mountains so you will be equipped with everything you will possibly need, you will also have two expert mountain climbers at your disposal and a very experienced doctor.'

'As from today your pay will be doubled and your wife will be well looked after despite her nationality being slightly suspect, we will overlook nothing and will give her a British passport together with police security at all times in your absence. With your knowledge of rough living in the wild in your youth, which we have checked, you are being made group leader of this expedition. We have contacted the local French resistance fighters in the area and they are expecting you soon.'

Mikael looked slightly bewildered at all this and was a bit lost for words, this was a bit more than he'd expected.

'When exactly will all this start then sir?'

Churchill smiled for the first time. 'Just as soon as you are all ready, the sooner the better, there is good weather expected two weeks from now. We already have people in the Alps making sure of the right location for you all it will be very secure and almost impossible to find by the enemy.'

Mikael looked more reassured by all this positive talk but he still hoped they were right and it was an achievable task. It was certainly different to painting ceilings.

Colonel Faversham then decided to conclude the meeting and wind up with his last few words. 'The most important thing for you all to remember is to wear your uniforms at all times. Otherwise you will be classed as spies and almost certainly shot. Is that clear?'

'Yes I understand sir. We will make sure of that.'

A smile came on the Prime Minister's face. 'Oh I almost forgot. Besides your linguistic talents you are, like me, an artist in your own right.'

Mikael nodded. He had heard that the man was a reasonably good painter as well as a politician.

The meeting ended with Colonel Faversham shaking his hand and wishing Mikael good luck in the mission.

It was some ten days later that Mikael was asked to report to an airfield called Tempsford in Bedfordshire for the flight that was to drop them in the French Alps. There he was to meet the three others an alpine guide, a wireless operator, and a doctor. At Tempsford they were to wait for the right weather for the drop which would be at night.

When he told Rosa later that day she cried bitterly for quite some time not knowing the full extent of the mission he was going on because of the secrecy of it. When she finally stopped crying he put his arms around her and decided to tell her the good parts of his new job.

'In a weeks time Rosa I have to leave and I may be gone a few months but before I leave we'll find a nice lady to help you with the house and baby. Also you'll find enough money in the bank each month to take care of all your bills while I'm away, I'll also leave you a telephone number to call should you need help in any way.'

'What do you mean Mikael, what sort of help?'

Mikael paused a moment. 'Well if the war gets any worse as it might well do some English people won't understand that you are married to an English army captain and that Italy is not on our side in this war.'

Rosa nodded. 'I understand Mikael. When I go shopping locally now some of the women around here make nasty remarks about me being a nasty Eytie, but I ignore them completely.'

'Good! Replied Mikael. 'And my job is so important that someone will be watching this house most of the time I'm gone to make sure that you are safe.'

Rosa seemed to cheer up at this statement but was still puzzled. 'How can we find someone in such a short time to help me with the baby Mikael?'

'Easy my love. I'll call an agency this afternoon and we'll have someone in a few days.'

'And what if she turns out to be no good what then?'

'You just call the agency and they will replace her.'

This seemed to satisfy Rosa and when they later booked a housekeeper who would help her with Rosanna she felt much better about Mikael leaving. The person booked was middle aged and also a good cook according to the agency.

The rest of the week passed very quickly and Mikael spent a lot of time at home knowing that maybe this would his last chance to be with them both for some months, possibly years.

The following week on June 22nd 1940 Mikael was picked up by an army car and driven to Tempsford airfield in readiness for their departure as soon as the weather was perfect for the drop. He was introduced to the rest of the crew and the talk was of that days fall of France to the Germans. This was indeed a blow, none of them thought it would happen so quickly. It was on that day that German troops entered Paris itself.

At the first evening's briefing they were given all the facts regarding the operation and told that the French resistance fighters were already preparing the place in the mountains for their headquarters. All over France the Germans were well dug in and in and had full control of every town and city, anyone resisting had been shot immediately. The situation was indeed grim and not likely to get any better for quite some time.

When the night of the operation arrived the sky was slightly cloudy with just a hint of a breeze, and they were surprised to learn that the weather was reasonably warm at the mountain drop off point. The aircraft laid on for them was the first Lysander Mikael had ever seen and the aircraft seemed small to him for such a journey, the inside was only just big enough take three passengers. It was obviously built to carry the crew only and any others had to sit on the floor wherever there was space.

Once started the aircraft taxied down the runway and took off with a huge deafening roar and lurched skywards, Mikael's heart was pounding thinking of what would happen once they were over France and within range of German guns. He was aware of the lack of heating inside the aircraft despite having ample clothing on and wondered if the temperature would drop once they were further south. His fears were justified. Within minutes it got much much colder, he glanced at the others nearby, they were also aware of the cold and showed it. Perhaps this was just a taste of what was to come in the Alps when they got there eventually. What amazed Mikael was the pilots skill at hovering over the sea when they approached the French coast to fool the German radar.

After what seemed like hours the sky was lit up like bonfire night when the German guns opened up on them as they reached central France, and the plane rocked violently as shells burst close to the it. It was over in minutes fortunately as they flew nearer the ground and the relief showed on all their faces. The Met Office forecast of light clouds over France was proving a godsend on this night trip. There was no more anti aircraft fire after that and they reached the target drop area without problems before midnight, and they prepared to leave the airccraft by the rear door.

As he looked earthwards Mikael shivered slightly as a sight of the snow capped mountain top was revealed by moonlight. As his parachute opened with a jerk he sensed the air getting slightly warmer, so that by the time he'd reached the ground near the bottom of the nearby mountain it was a different world. As they gathered the chutes together the rest of their equipment started to fall around them but by then help arrived in the form of French resistance men who collected the stores and led them to the secret hideaway.

As they approached the concealed entrance about a mile up the mountain track there was nothing at all to reveal just where this place was and how big it was inside, It was absolutely massive once past the huge boulder shielding the cave itself which was in an unlit state. The leader of the French men assured them the Germans would never find this place and even if they did could almost certainly not think of attacking it. It was above a slope that was only passable in small numbers and they had a large gun concealed above the entrance that could hold off a regiment of foot troops. This gun had been used to great effect during a previous war and killed many invaders trying to gain access to the cave.

Once inside they were astounded to find a huge amount of extra food and stores already laid out neatly for them, plus a small amount of medical equipment and fuel for keeping the place warm. Little did any of them realize just how long they were going to spend in this hideaway helping others to escape the Germans. This place was going to be their home for much longer than any of them could even guess at, it was about to change their lives and others forever.

After unpacking a few bits of personal belongings they all sat down to introduce themselves during a quick meal prepared by the four resistance men. As leader Mikael started the ball rolling as his French was he thought probably slightly better than some of the others.

'I'm Captain Mikael Garodny and my job mainly is to be the interpretor for this group during our stay here but I have been trained briefly in mountain climbing, skiing, and basic first aid.' He then pointed to his colleague closest to him dressed in army uniform. 'And this man is Captain Charles Moorcroft who is our medical doctor and whom we are relying on for the more serious first aid.' Charles grins at this statement as he is also a qualified surgeon. Mikael then moves on to the next member of his group.

'Our next lucky member is from the Royal Air Force and is Flight Lieutenant John Bremner and is in charge of our radio equipment. And last but not least Sergeant Bruce Johnson, our own Alpine Guide who has had years of experience, I'm told climbing these mountains over the years.'

Mikael then waved the French men to start their introductions. With a smile on his face he felt his French translation had gone down reasonably well. He just hoped that all his interpretations would be be equally understood by everyone, because some of the dialects in this region were a bit quaint he'd been told.

The tallest of the Frenchmen then stood up, he certainly was a tough looking character and one not to upset or pick a fight with. He started with his own name Jean Paul Gautier and he had just lost nearly all his family in a nearby village when the Germans occupied it, they'd shot almost everyone there. He said that he'd nothing more to lose and that killing the Germans was a pleasure he'd pursue for the duration of the war. He then introduced the next man as Louis Gilbert who was much smaller but a happier looking person, his role was looking after the guns they had acquired from the Germans. He was also reputed to be an expert with a knife when a silent killing was required and this had been quite often.

The next man introduced himself in reasonable English, his name was Pierre Armand and his mother was English and his role was that of guide and an expert skier together with Pascal Simon the man next to him, who was their explosives expert. Pierre went on to say that between them they'd caused havoc with the Germans over the last few months so much, and that they were on the wanted list by the Gestapo.

Then Mikael explained the purpose of the trip and set about finding out just how many allied personnel had passed through the district so far. There was no dispute about each ones role in this operation, the French were to find the allied military personnel, and Mikael's group were to look after them when they arrived at the cave. They were also to arrange evacuation where possible by air back to England.

Later, after the Frenchmen had left them the rest of the day was spent checking the stores and looking around at the enormous cave that they were to spend a lot of time in. It was really out of this world and a real tourist attraction with enough room to hold at least a hundred people without overcrowding, the only drawback being the temperature. But they soon get used to it and the weather outside was getting warmer each day. It was just a case of taking it in turn to keep watch outside, just in case any stray German troops wandered around the base of the mountain.

Mikael's knowledge of wild edible plants was now going to be a big addition to their diet and help to make their stores go further, his companions soon became adept at finding enough each day to keep them healthy. It was fortunate that they soon took to this way of living and there was an occasional rabbit or mountain goat as a luxury that passed their way.

It was some weeks before there was any activity by the French partisans and it came as a bit of a shock to the group to see some of the injuries in the wounded troops they brought in to them to sort out. At first it was a trickle then after that at least ten a day would arrive and the doctor Charles Moorcroft was kept busy attending their injuries assisted by whoever was free at the time. This task fell mainly to Mikael as Bruce Johnson spent most days guiding the fit ones to the next group of partisans some distance away across the mountain pass.

It was quite an experience assisting the doctor Charles in some of the more serious operations especially as he'd never seen such wounds close up ever before. He knew that he'd never be able to cope himself without a real physician in these circumstances and it just might possibly get worse as the war progressed, the thought of what could happen really worried him.

Most nights were spent discussing with the others the state of the war's progress, as news came in through the wounded troops and the French Partisans. They painted a grim picture of just what was happening in the country around them. So far the Germans hadn't shown up anywhere near them and hopefully this was going to continue, the French were keeping them posted of their nearby movements. Knowing the Germans were keeping careful track of all radio signals, John their radio operator used the radio for only vital signals to England during the early hours and even then very briefly.

The weeks went by very quickly and the casualties were coming in very spasmodically but they were kept quite busy, food was supplemented with herbs and odd animals gathered by them each on a regular basis. They took it in turns to cook trying not to show too much smoke in the process just in case the odd German trooper should spot it. With Italy now in the war their troops might have ideas of helping their Allies in this area quite close to the border. Mikael wondered how this turn of events might be affecting Rosa and daughter Rosanna who was now seven years old. He was hoping that the men at the Foreign Office were living up to their strict promise to look after them both.

Chapter Forty Two

The Blitz

It was early September whilst Rosa was awaiting the arrival of Rosanna from school with her nanny Maria that she heard the wail of the air raid sirens. This was not an unusual sound as it was a very frequent occurrence at the time, mostly with nothing much happening, but this time she felt slightly uneasy as she went out in the garden. From her view there on top of Hampstead Heath the sky seemed quite dark looking south over London as though a storm was imminent. Within a few minutes the reason was clear the whole sky was full of aircraft and the sound was horrendous even before the bombs started to fall. Then nearby anti aircraft guns opened up to make further noise. She glanced nervously at her watch and moved quickly to the front door and opened it knowing Rosanna should be back at this time, and she was normally never ever late.

Time passed and it was a further fifteen minutes before they both appeared at the end of the drive by which time Rosa was going out of her mind with worry. She moved quickly forward and glancing angrily at Maria took her daughter's hand and rushed her into the house. Once inside she spoke loudly to Maria who looked slightly nervously at her.

'Where have you both been!' She shouted. 'Can't you see there's an air raid going on? I've been so worried Maria.'

Maria looked nervous she knew her employer was subject to nervous tantrums at the slightest upset so she thought it wise not to argue with her.

'Sorry madam! We just stopped a few minutes to look at the flowers on the way back that's all.'Maria glanced at Rosanna who nodded. 'That's right mother we weren't very late were we.?'

Rosa seemed to cool down a little at this point and they went into the kitchen for afternoon tea.

Later that night when Rosanna was safely tucked up in bed Rosa left Maria to watch her while she went out into the back garden to see the fires burning all over London. This suddenly ceased at just after six o'clock, but after a lull of a few hours when it got dark another wave of German bombers arrived to drop their deadly cargo where the incendiary fires were still alight. As the sound of the falling bombs grew much louder Rosa decided that she would waken Rosanna, and together with Maria they would go to the nearest tube station shelter. She had been told that the Hampstead one was probably the safest one in London being the deepest but she certainly didn't want to sleep there herself.

Gathering a few blankets and a pillow for the child who was still only half awake they walked quickly to the station but were stopped at the entrance by a very officious air raid warden, he told them it was already full and had been since six o/clock. This was a bit of a shock to Rosa as she was a bit reluctant to mix with all the strange people she'd seen sleeping on the platforms anyway. Belsize Park station was too far to walk to with the sound of the bombs going off in the near distance.
Retracing their way back home quickly Rosa decided that her best bet would be to use the wine cellar, it was probably better than trying to get in the underground before it got full each night. By the time they reached home Rosanna was really getting agitated and sobbing loudly, but it didn't take long to get her back to sleep in the quiet cellar away from the sound of the falling bombs.

Petra opened her post the next morning expecting the usual bills and was pleasantly surprised to find a short letter from Mickael which had obviously been well censored judging by the official stamp marks on it. He wrote that he was in good health and reasonably safe but couldn't say where he was at present and just in case his mail wasn't reaching Rosa to tell her he was O.K. She wiped the tears away from her eyes and glanced at his portrait on the shelf nearby and hoped that wherever he was he'd come home safely soon.

Life had changed dramatically for both her and Charles over the past few years as it had for most of their friends, but at least they had managed to get by without the help of servants. Charles was now in Winston Churchill's cabinet as treasury adviser and was now working long hours, but at least his workplace had a proper air raid shelter in it unlike most of the buildings in London. The dreadful bombing had by now been going on all night and the damage was horrendous especially in the east end and the dock area. It was reported that many hundreds had been killed and huge fires were still burning all over London.

Apart from keeping the house in order she now spent a lot of time helping in the London Hospital doing just about anything that was needed in the catering department. It was a nightmare trying to keep the supplies there organized most of the time as the farms that served them previously were very short of help, most of the farmhands were now in the forces. Petra, although still very healthy realizes that at the age of sixty two she really aught to ease up a little and stop working soon, but felt that life at home alone was not for her just yet. With her other children all settled and married she felt satisfied with life in general and that hopefully nothing would go wrong, unfortunately life is very unpredictable as she soon found out.

Chapter Forty Three

The Lodgers

It was some months later that Petra received news from her relations Olga and Yuri in France that there was a problem at the farm where they were staying. It seemed that the owner who had previously promised them a share in it was now going back on his word, having had their help in getting it going. His attitude was to let them do all the work and he was getting the benefit without lifting a finger. There was also trouble in being harassed by the Germans on a daily basis taking their crops and produce whenever they wanted them. They were seriously thinking of trying to leave the country somehow and returning to England, but this looked a formidable task. The children now grown up didn't want to leave anyway so could she speak to Charles about accommodation if they should succeed in reaching England?

Later that evening when Charles came home Petra waited until after dinner before tackling him about Olga and Yuri's problem. She more or less knew what he'd say before she spoke but had to satisfy herself that he'd approve.

'Charles I've had a message from Mikael and he says he's alright but still not letting us know just where he is.'

Charles smiled at this remark. 'Of course he can't tell you that. It's because in case the Germans find out where people are.'

Petra nodded. 'Yes I understand that but it's difficult just not knowing what exactly he's doing. And I've heard from Olga and Yuri in France and they are having problems on the farm and are thinking about trying to get over to England if they can.'

'You have to be joking of course.' Charles replied. 'Even I couldn't manage that trip at the present time.'

Petra paused and smiled. 'I'm sure you could dear if you tried. Do you remember a while back when they left England you said that if anything went wrong in France for them they could stay here?'

Charles looked at her cautiously.

'Yes I did but things have changed a bit since then and with no servants left here it could be a bit awkward. Mind you the mews flat is empty, that's if you think it's good enough for them?'

Petra smiled this was more than she'd hoped for. 'Thank you Charles. The mews flat would be great for them until they find a place to live, I'm sure they'd love it and please god they find a way out of France with all that fighting going on.'

It was quite some months later that Petra opened the front door to answer the bell and saw her two relations standing there with bundles of possessions looking haggard and weary. Tears of joy rolled down her face as she greeted them both and she hurried them inside. She showed them into the lounge and started to question them. 'How did you manage to get out of France?'

Olga and Yuri smiled and glanced at each other. 'It was bribery that did it mostly and now we are broke.' Said Yuri. 'It took most of our savings and once we'd reached the French coast we followed what you did all those years, ago and rowed across in an old boat we bought for a few francs. It took much longer than we thought and at one time we were spotted by the Germans but they thought we were fishing. But when they saw we had no fish they just wished us luck and left.'

'So you didn't need passports then?' Said Petra.

'No! And that might be problem in England?' He answered.

Petra shook her head. 'No don't worry, my husband will take care of that. He will make sure you are taken care of. And when you've eaten I will take you to the flat that will be your home for as long as you want.'

Chapter Forty Four

1942

Mikael woke with a start. Someone was moving on the path outside. It was just beginning to show daylight through the cave's entrance and Bruce Johnson should have been on guard outside to warn them of any problems. He eased himself quickly from his makeshift bed, moved quickly to the spyhole above the cave door and looked out at the path below. Where was Bruce that he hadn't spotted the two German soldiers making their way up the path? Grabbing his pistol he went back for another look, they were now nearing the entrance. One pointed upwards he'd obviously spotted what looked like the disguised entrance and drew his gun.

Mikael didn't wait any longer. The situation could be nasty should they alert others, he didn't hesitate but shot them both through the spyhole. They both fell sideways down the path and lay dead.

He moved outside quickly to see what had happened to Bruce the others now awake followed him shouting questions.

'Help me get these two inside one of you, what's happened to Bruce. He should have warned us they were coming.'

John Bremner then got hold of the first German soldier and he and Mikael hauled him inside the cave, and then returned for the other one. Their next task was to search for Bruce who they found on the lower slope bleeding from knife wounds, and half conscious.

The Germans must have left him for dead some time beforehand. John quickly checked him over just before he regained consciousness. They carried him carefully back to the cave where Charles got to work on the wounds after first giving him a painkiller injection. Mikael took the binoculars outside to scour the surrounding area for signs of other German troops in the area. It was strange that only two soldiers were alone up in the mountain area, and they must surely be soon missed.

The rest of the morning was spent carefully burying the two German bodies, and removing all traces of blood outside in case more troops came searching for their comrades. Bruce when fully recovered could only remember hearing footsteps in the dark then nothing more after that. Leaving Charles tending to Bruce's wounds Mikael and John once again went outside to check if there where any sign of other troops in the area but there were none to their relief. Mikael glanced around the rocky area.

'We seem to be running out of places to bury anything around here now John?'

John nodded. 'That's right! There's so many arms and leg parts under these rocks the worms must be having a ball.'

Mikael had stopped counting how many amputations he'd helped Charles do in the past eighteen months, there must have been dozens of them.

There followed a few days of inactivity until two of the resistance fighters showed up with an urgent warning. They said that the two soldiers had been missed and a search party was beginning to comb the area for them. An overnight plane pick up had to be arranged urgently and the French would cover the cave entrance properly after removing all traces of their stay there. Radio contact was made and the weather forecast was favourable for that nights landing. Fortunately there was a full moon due as the aircraft had limited navigation equipment.

They cleared out all the reasonably light equipment then said farewell to their brave French helpers, and with a guide to lead made their way slowly around the mountain to arrive early at the temporary landing spot four kilometres away. On arrival they met the Partisans who'd set out the cleared runway for them and were equipped with torches waiting for darkness to guide the aircraft in. They then waited what seemed like hours during which Mikael closed his eyes and tried to think of just how many personnel they'd helped back to England during their time there, it must have been hundreds altogether. He just prayed that they would get back home now safely without being shot down by the German guns over France.

As darkness came the sound of a distant aircraft was heard coming towards them, it then circled the area twice before a bumpy landing along the well lit grassy runway. Within minutes they were on board with all the equipment stowed in the hold. Mikael was the last to leave having thanked their French guide and his team for their help, at this point he was hanged a large envelope to take back to England containing maps of the area.

Once airborne the flight back went reasonably well until just north of Paris when anti aircraft shells started to explode all around them, the plane rocked heavily for a few minutes, but there were no direct hits fortunately. As they reached the French coast two German fighters were sighted well below, but they didn't intercept them for some reason. It was after midnight when they landed at Tempsford airfield and they were driven to their quarters for the night very tired, but still buzzing from the fact that they were now safely back in England. The priority was to have the luxury of a bath and toilet something they'd not seen for a long time. Later in the officers mess having a meal, Mikael had a conversation with the pilot of the aircraft that brought them back. He said that it was just one of many missions he had flown in the last year and probably wouldn't be the last.

Next morning they were called to a short meeting with the commanding officer of the base, and told they were to be driven to Whitehall for a debriefing by Ministry Officials. Then they could be going home if all went well. Mikael showed the maps he'd been given and was told to pass them to the chiefs of staff in London. Outside a large car was waiting with their kit inside and within minutes they were on their way to London, their feelings were like being in a different world from their primitive cave dwelling.

On arrival at the Foreign Office they were shown to an upstairs large office where Mikaels previous contacts Lord Carlyle and Captain Philips were present. After being greeted they were asked to be seated before the meeting started, not knowing that somebody else was also very interested in the proceedings.

'Thank you Gentlemen! For the fantastic work you have done in

France on our behalf.' Said Lord Carlyle. 'And before we start I want to introduce the man responsible for what he calls his secret army which you have been part of .'

At that point an inner door opened and in walked the beaming Prime Minister Winston Churchill, who then proceeded to shake their hands warmly before speaking.

'Good morning! You are here today at my request, mainly to thank you for your sterling rescue work for us in difficult circumstances over the last year. Unknown to you some of those that you saved have since not only recovered fully, but have helped us tremendously in many ways. You have been part of what is known as Special Operations, these operate in many parts of the world, and has produced some amazing results. You were brought back very quickly knowing how close you were to being discovered and we could possibly want to use that base again sometime.

We have been informed that most of the nearby villagers were sadly shot by the Germans when the two troopers didn't return to their barracks. But this has been happening for a long time in France and they have sadly carried on trying to live as normal a life as possible. It is due to your skill and perseverance that from right under the noses of the German army, you have managed to help save the lives of countless men and women. So as some consolation for you efforts you are free from duty and can return home for the rest of the year with our blessing. There may be something for you to take part in next year, but we shall have to wait and see how the war progresses.

Before you go I must impress on you that your operation must be kept secret even from your close relatives to ensure the safety of the many personnel working around the world at this time. Thank you gentlemen. That will be all.'

The Prime Minister then left the room leaving Lord Carlyle to call the meeting to a halt, and the three of them left in an unmarked car to be taken to their respective homes.

Chapter Forty Five

Home Again

As the car stopped at Mikael's request a few yards from his house, he took leave of his companions and carried his kit to the front door. Although he had a key somewhere in his luggage he pushed the front doorbell hoping that someone was in. He waited quite some time for an answer before the curtain moved and he saw a young woman looking in his direction, then after a pause she opened the door.

'Hello!' She said. 'Can I help you?'

Taken aback Mikael couldn't believe that this person just didn't know who he was. 'Well yes. I am Mikael the owner, home on leave, is my wife in?'

'Well no. She is out at present but should be back soon. But please come in she wasn't expecting you today, at least she didn't say so.'

Mikael picked up his kitbag and followed the woman into the house and he walked into the lounge and sat down looking rather puzzled.

The woman looked at the framed picture on the wall and could see that he was indeed the owner and better explain who she was.

'Sorry to be so cautious, but I've only been here a short while and it was a shock to see you standing there outside. My name is Helen, and I'm the housekeeper for your wife. Would you like something to drink?'

Mikael smiled for the first time that day. 'Yes of course a coffee would be most welcome thank you.'

Helen left him there while she prepared his drink in the kitchen, he looked around and noted a few small changes to the place. One of the most noticeable was the heavy curtains and sticky tape across the large windows. This was obviously there to stop the blast of bombs showering glass all over the place. The room itself wasn't quite as tidy as he'd remembered it previously, as though it wasn't used much. He wondered how his wife had spent the time he'd been away during the heavy bombing of London, although there wasn't much sign of damage in the Hampstead area.

When Helen returned with his coffee he decided to tactfully question her a little.

'Thank you Helen.' He said taking it from her. 'Where is my daughter this afternoon?'

'In school until I go and fetch her shortly. She replied nervously. She will be glad to see you sir, she's always talking about you.'

'And my wife. where is she today, shopping?'
Helen paused a moment. Well not really she goes to a tea dance today.'

'And what's that then?' Mikael asked.

'Well. It's a once a week meeting to keep the overseas troops morale up, or so they say.'

Mikael didn't like the thought of his wife mixing with servicemen without him being there, but he decided to speak to her later about this.

Helen glanced at the clock and was relieved to see it was time to leave for the school to pick up Rosanna, and avoid answering awkward questions about her mistress. She left Mikael seated there with all sorts of thoughts about his wife and what she had been up to in his absence. He decided to go upstairs and shower and change into more relaxing clothes in order to greet his wife when she returned home.

After he'd finished he returned downstairs just as his daughter Rosanna come in from school, she flew into his arms with tears of joy running down her cheeks.

'You're home at last, daddy, I'm so glad you are back. We've missed you so much.'

Mikael hugged her for quite some minutes his little girl hadn't changed at all. She was still the same loving child he'd left behind in what seemed years ago.

He put her down and hand in hand they went into the lounge where he eyed her up and down at arms length.

'My you have grown quickly. You are nearly as big as me already. Come and sit down and tell me what you've been up to while I've been away.'

Rosanna looked sad. 'Well the war has been awful so far and the bombs have been nearly every night. Some of my school friends have lost their houses, they are living with relations mostly. Sometimes we don't get to sleep at nights. And it's so cold in our cellar that I just lie there shivering. Perhaps now that you're home we can get some coal to light the fires like we used to.'

Mikael looked at his daughter and hoped that he could spend some time watching her grow up, perhaps now was the time to make life a little easier for his family. And where's mummy today Rosanna?

'Oh at one of her silly tea dances I suppose. That's all she talks about just lately. And uncle Teddy.'

Mikaels face changed. And who's he then?'

'He's an American army officer who stayed with us when they told us to house a few soldiers, because we had a big house.'

'And how long did he stay here then?'

'Oh just a few weeks. Now he's in a posh hotel in the west end.'

'And does mummy still see him then?'

'Sometimes. When he's not busy.'

'And who else stayed here then?'

'Some Canadian officers as well.'

Mikael didn't like the sound of all these goings on. This was not what he'd expected from his very loving wife. She seemed to have been living it up whilst he'd been away. She would have some explaining to do when she arrived back home. He looked at the clock wondering when Rosa would return, meanwhile after having a meal he tried questioning Rosanna about her mother's lifestyle. She wasn't very forthcoming however and slightly nervous about something. She did let slip the fact that her mother had visited a doctor in Brighton a few months ago and that she'd been very ill on the way back home. This resulted in a visit to the local hospital where they kept her in for three days. Her mother never did explain what it was for but it took weeks for her to recover fully.

Mikael was shocked at this information and could only guess at the cause of the trouble. It sounded like a pregnancy termination without a doubt, and it certainly wasn't caused by him. This was indeed something he wasn't expecting and his mind was in a whirl, just how was he going to cope with it, supposing it was true? He tried to put it out of his mind for the moment but it wouldn't go away. What had happened to the innocent girl he'd married all those years ago?

It was some hours later that Rosa came in smiling and on seeing Mikael was more than surprised but within seconds rushed to embrace him.

'Why didn't you let me know you were coming Mikael?'

'I couldn't' he replied. We weren't told until this morning.'

'You look so thin Mikael. Not a bit like when you left.'

He paused wondering what to say next. This was not the way he should be feeling now, he decided to wait until later to question her about what Rosanna had told him.

'You look different too Rosa. Has the war been bad for you?'

She edged away from him nervously. 'Sometimes. But it's the nights that are the worst especially when the bombs are falling. And so many people have been killed since you've been gone. But what about you. Where have you been , or can't you say?'

Mikael shook his head. 'No I can't. It's part of my job and something that maybe I'll tell you about when the war is over.'

Mikael looked at her wondering whether this was the time to speak about her wartime entertaining of allied troops, but decided to wait for a better moment. After all he had months ahead of him to find out just what

Rosa had been up to. Perhaps he was misjudging her without any proof that she had misbehaved in any way. He had to find some painting work to pass the time until the next mission, if there was to be one.

Later he inspected his workshop studio at the top of the house and found it exactly as he'd left it. He knew that to achieve his lifelong ambition of painting a masterpiece, he'd have to spend more time not only planning it, but many years executing it. He was an expert at restoration of other people's work, of that there was no doubt, but this wasn't enough for him. So he set about visiting large churches with suitable ceilings hoping to find perhaps one to work on.

Without spending too much time on this search for a suitable church Mikael did eventually find one, which, although slightly smaller than he wanted, was almost right. The problem was then getting all the proper permissions from the church committee This took longer than he'd expected and meantime he took on a few small art jobs to pass the time. It was fortunate that the the building of his choice was not too far from London.

During this period Rosa had become accustomed to her husband being home, and although it restricted her movements somewhat she knew that until he went away again, this was how she would have to behave. It was only a few months later that she annoyingly discovered that she was pregnant, and telling Mikael this worried her slightly. But the news seemed to please him although he was worried about her having another child at her age.

Trying not to disclose too much, Mikael had very long discussions with his daughter Rosanna about the war in general and described in detail the sufferings of the men injured in battle. Of course he never mentioned exactly where he'd been during his absence. She noticed that during these times alone with him his hands would shake a little, not seriously but just enough to worry her slightly. It was during these moments alone with Rosanna, that Mikael tried to find out just what his wife had been up to whilst he'd been away. She avoided giving away all that she knew for fear of upsetting her parents marriage. But Mikael managed to get just enough information to piece together the fact that his wife had definitely been unfaithful. The fact that she was about to give birth to his child made him reluctant to have it out with her, certainly not before the the child was born anyway.

During the following months it preyed on Mikael's mind so much that he started drinking quite heavily, just a few whiskies at first then it became a bottle a day. He excused himself by thinking it was just a passing phase in his life, and that this was part of the healing process from his dangerous activities in the mountains. But this just didn't happen, he soon became addicted to the drink and it was showing in his work. He had to abandon the church project which was something he'd never done before, and made all sorts of excuses to get out of the project. He decided to go and see his mother and see if she could help him in any way.

His mother was pleased to see him although it was the second time he'd been there since his return, and she was a little shocked at his appearance. He looked a lot older, and haggard. As he hugged her on the doorstep she took a deep breath and waited until they were inside before speaking.

'Whatever have you been up to Mikael?' She said. You look terrible.'

'It's life in general mother. Everything seems to be going wrong since I've got back. I'll tell you in a minute, but how is life with you?'

Petra looked at him without a hint of a smile on her face. She should have been pleased to see him, but not like this.

'We are all well fortunately despite the war and I still find plenty to do. But what's gone wrong for you Mikael?'

Mikael looked at his mother grimly. 'It's everything mother but mainly Rosa, she's changed and doesn't seem the same person I first married.

'In what way Mikael?

'She's been unfaithful mother. I'm almost certain of that.'

Petra looked stunned at this, it wasn't something she'd been expecting at all. Rosa did after all come from a very religious family. 'How did you find out?'

'By some of the things Rosanna has told me, what Rosa has been up to while I've been gone.'

Petra paused a moment before answering. The implication of what he'd told her was now beginning to sink in. 'But you said only last week that she was having another child. How does that fit in with what you've just said?'

'I'm not really sure that it's mine mother.'

Petra's mouth dropped instantly, she stood there dumbfounded this was totally unexpected. A thing like this had never happened in her family before. 'What are you going to do then Mikael?'

'I'll just wait until the child is born, then decide whether to question her about things. I'm not absolutely positive yet in my mind, but it really is bothering me that strangers have slept in my house while I've been away.'

Petra looked astonished at Mikael wondering how he could be so calm about this nasty situation, she would certainly never have allowed it to happen to her. But what advice should she give him?

'Rosanna did tell me that the authorities billeted some airmen in your house Mikael, so that wasn't your wife's fault surely?'

'Maybe but what happened after could be. Only time will tell. I don't want to implicate Rosanna because Rosa might try and take it out on her for telling me things.'

Mikael left his mothers house feeling just slightly better, she did have a way of calming the situation and making him a little more confident about his task ahead. On the way home by tube he couldn't help noticing how many young couples looked so happy and contented in each others company. It wasn't so long ago he was in the same position. Now it seemed to have all changed, his life seemed full of uncertainties.

Back home Rosa sat there thinking of just what had gone wrong with her life since the war had started, and Mikael had been taken away from her. The temptation of living a better life had been too much for her when the airmen had been in her house. They were obviously lonely away from home and during their off duty times were looking for brief moments of respite from their duties. At the time to her it seemed like mild flirtation, but some passionate moments led to serious lovemaking on more than one occasion. Mikael had tried to question her about her activities but she mainly fobbed him off with feeble answers that didn't reveal much of what had really happened. She knew that he wasn't convinced in any way by the look on his face and he seemed to go into a bad mood for days. Things were never going to be the same again. If he ever found out she'd had an abortion that would be almost certainly be the end of their marriage, so she prayed this would never happen.

Rosanna was spending more and more time with her father, and not only talking with him but having the occasional drink as well. And although she was taking in most of the things he spoke about some of it was slightly beyond her. One of the strange things that she discovered was that he had three passports in his bedside drawer, and when questioned about them he said that he'd had them years. How she wondered could he be English, French, and Italian all at the same time? This seemed very strange to her especially as she didn't own one herself. She decided to push her luck a little and try and get one for herself.

'Do you think it's possible for me to have a passport one day father?' She asked him.

'What would you want it for, Rosanna?'

'I'd like to go abroad and visit places like France and Italy on my bike.'

Mikael smiled, this from such a young girl seemed crazy but who knows? Perhaps she could, she certainly was a very determined girl.

Mikael looked at her thoughtfully. 'Perhaps when you leave school and the war is over then I'll think about it. And how is school by the way, do you still like it?'

Rosanna grimaced. 'No I hate it. And those horrible nuns with their vicious canes frighten me, and they are always picking on me just because I have a foreign name.'

Mikael didn't like the sound of this from Rosanna, she was usually quite easy going and not upset by trivial matters.

'Tell me next time something happens and I'll come up and talk to these nuns. This school costs quite a lot of money and you shouldn't be treated any different from the others.'

Rosanna nodded although she didn't want her father to be bothered with her problems. But it was nice to know he cared that much, and with only two years left at school she' stick it out somehow. Little did she know how these years would change their lives forever.

Chapter Forty Six

April 1945

It was just a few months later that Mikael was contacted by the Foreign Office with details of his next assignment. Although he'd not fully recovered from the previous one he was aware that the war was still in progress, and they might need him again. Just how to tell his family and still keep it secret where he was going was a problem. The complexity of this mission was mind blowing to Mikael when it was explained to him, he didn't think it possible to carry out just what they wanted. His mission was to find just where Benito Mussolini was located before the partisans got hold of him. The powers that be wanted him badly for a war trial and a public execution was not on the agenda of the allies. If he succeeded it would be major triumph and no expense was to spared.

Mikael was first grilled extensively by top linguists about his knowledge of the peasant Italian language, just to make sure nobody would suspect him of being a foreigner. He passed with flying colours and within days was being dropped with the right clothes and a radio operator companion at a small airfield, near a village in the vicinity of Mussolini's last known sighting.

It took just a few days to mingle with the locals before he got word of a party of strangers living in a large house on the edge of the village. As dusk came they moved on to the house and kept watch from a distance as five people inside moved around. Round the back partly out of sight was an old battered army lorry with German markings on it. This was the only vehicle present and seemed to be the only means of escape should it be needed. Mikael moved towards the house shielded by the bushes and lay watching the inmates move around. It took only minutes to establish that Mussolini was one of them, and he quickly returned to his companion. Within minutes a radio message was passed to England and a squad of nearby S.A.S. men ordered to seize the occupants. The instructions were to wait away from the house at the far end of the drive for the arrival of these men. It was only a few minutes before the sound of a lorry was heard, and it passed them quickly heading for the house. The gunshots followed by lots of shouting and the lorry returned full of people. Mikael obviously thought the mission was successful, but wondered how they were going to return home.

Suddenly they were aware that there were soldiers all around them and realized they were British. The officer in charge spoke first.

'How many are there in the house?'

Mikael looked at him amazed. 'I thought you knew. Didn't you just take them away in a lorry?'

The officer shook his head. 'No we've only just arrived, seems as if we're too late, but we'd better check the house out.'

He sent two of his men to make sure the place was empty, they returned within minutes and confirmed this to be the case.

'Damm! The partisans have beaten us to it this time. They obviously wanted them more than we did. You two had better come with us and we'll arrange for your pick up back to blighty. Sorry to put you to all this trouble but we can't win them all.' He paused with a puzzled look on his face.

'I've been told you knew Mussolini well, how did that happen?'

Mikael looked slightly embarrassed at this point.

'Oh I did some work for him a few years ago, that's all. A bit of painting in Rome on one of the government buildings.'

The officer smiled at this. 'I hope you got paid for the work? I don't think you'll get the chance of seeing him alive again, not after that lot are finished with him.'

The trip back home was a relief and Mikael thanked his lucky stars they had got out of this mission unharmed, it could have been quite nasty had they interfered.

Back home again the the following morning, the Times newspaper reported the assassination of Benito Mussolin, and his mistress Clara Pettacci, by Italian partisans. Mikael stared at the front page wondering how different the story would have been had they arrived a few minutes sooner. But that was war, and very few things turned out the way governments planned them. A few days later Italy surrendered followed by Germany after bitter battles throughout the whole of Europe, and Russia. It was good to be back home with his family, knowing that he'd probably not be needed again for any military purposes. Now Mikael could settle down and live a quiet artistic life once again, but he felt somehow uneasy because he not only still held the rank of Captain, but also was on the army payroll as well. The original contract for five years that he'd been promised was soon due to expire, so he looked forward to the time he could hand in his army uniform.

His anticipated quiet return was interrupted by Rosa's sudden medical problems. Her arms both started to swell dangerously with no previous symptoms at all, Mikael took her to the doctors straight away, and after examining her thoroughly. He said that she most likely had copper poisoning. Mikael looked at Rosa wondering how she could have got this.

'What have you been up to Rosa?' He asked with a serious look on his face.

Rosa shrugged. 'It must have been when we worked in the munitions factory a couple of years ago. We had a lot of copper there usually, but we did wash our hands after work always.'

The doctor nodded. 'That would explain it, we've had a few patients with it lately.' He wrote a few notes then stood up.

'First I need you Mrs Garodny to go to the casualty department of the Royal Free Hospital and they will treat this very easily. But before that I need to speak to you Mr Garodny privately, so can you leave us a minute please Madam.'

Rosa looked at her husband nervously wondering just what the doctor wanted, perhaps he was going to tell him of her medical problems. She hoped this was not so, she then stood up and slowly left the room. Mikael sensed that something was about to be revealed he suspected for quite some time but hoped he was wrong.

The doctor looked very serious when he started to speak quietly.

'I understand that you have been away for some of the war Mr Garodny?'

Mikael nodded. 'Yes I have!'

'And did your wife tell you about her miscarriage?'

'No but my daughter did.'

'Then I must warn you that because of the damage that the quack abortionist she visited did to her, she will be very lucky to have any more children.'Mikael stared at him without speaking for a few seconds, his mind was in a whirl he then blurted out.

'But she's pregnant now. Do you think she''ll be alright doctor?'

'Maybe! Only time will tell, I hope so for your sake. Make sure you tell them at the hospital when she gets there, they will need to know that. Let me know if there are any problems won't you?'

Mikael looked terrible at this news, he would now have to face up to reality and talk seriously to his wife. He nodded. 'Of course I will doctor.'

As he left the room and met Rosa outside, she just knew from the sad look on his face, that he knew what had happened to her whilst he'd been away. Once outside and on the way to the hospital Rosa spoke first. 'Well! What did the doctor have to say Mikael?'

He looked at her and in a lowered voice said. 'He told me that you had a termination a year ago. What have you got to say to explain that?'

Rosa looked away not knowing what to say. 'I'm so sorry Mikael. While you were gone I was so lonely at times, and wondering if you'd ever come back.'

'And I thought that you were quite a different person Rosa, and to me our marriage was a sacred thing. You have really disappointed me, and I hope to god the child you are carrying is definitely mine?'

'Yes of course it is Mikael. I'm only three months over.'

When they eventually reached the hospital it was only a short wait to see a doctor who specialised in skin problems. He said that this was quite a common complaint for women who'd been working in factories. He gave her a prescription for two lots of ointment and a blood test and said it would clear up within weeks, if not to go back to her G.P. Mikael wondered why it was that their doctor couldn't have done the same?

On their walk back home Rosa stopped suddenly and clutched at a park bench before sitting on it white faced,she then burst into tears. Mikael was taken aback at this and sat next to her putting his arm around her. It was quite some time before she stopped crying and spoke.

'I'm so sorry Mikael! While you were gone life has been awful here lots of my friends have been killed in the bombing, and everything seems to have gone wrong. We have been so cold in the winter that most folk around here raid the cellars of bombed buildings for coal. Our subways are always full with people sleeping there to avoid the bombs, and to get a place there is impossible after three in the afternoon. And both Maria and I had to work at the munitions factory for the first year you were away.

Mikael looked at her intently, after what he'd been through abroad recently this was nothing, but he felt a little sympathy for her at this time but she did after all have Maria to help her. The tears were now starting to subside and Rosa wiped the last few from her eyes and sniffed. 'The worst thing of all were those horrid men from the government watching me night and day as though I were a criminal. I know they were there to look after me but it' as though I was being spied on all the time.'

'Well it's probably all over now Rosa, things will get better, you'll see. And hopefully I shan't be needed any more.'

Mikael held out his hand to help her up. 'Come on then lets go home.'

This was the time to forgive and move on, because during the last few years he'd learnt that life itself was a precious thing and could end at a moments notice.

Chapter Forty Seven

Peace 1946

This was the year that things really changed for Mikael and Rosa. after the birth of their second child a boy that they named Thomas. Everything seemed at first to be going well, until Rosanna was expelled from the convent for what the nuns called insolence and disobedience. It seemed that she was sent to the chapel to ask gods forgiveness for something trivial, but after staying there quite some time she was unable to do this as she couldn't see him. This of course was only part of the story, and she told her father that she hated the place anyway, and wasn't learning anything there.

Once home all day there were continual rows with her equally stubborn mother, who seemed to think she should look after the new baby full time. The outcome of this was that Mikael not only found Rosanna a bedsit in a Hampstead house, but an apprenticeship with a first class ladies dressmaker in the West End. This seemed to work well and she learned a lot, but within a year she pleaded with her father to get her a passport for her cycle ride to France and Italy. She hated working seated for hours at a time doing what she thought was boring needlework for rich ladies who didn't appreciate the work put into these clothes.

It was on the night that she next visited her father that the real opportunity came to tackle him about her trip abroad. He seemed to be in a good mood when she arrived, so after taking him a cup of tea she sat down near to him smiling. Mikael sensed something was on her mind and studied her intently before speaking.

'You look happy today Rosanna have you got some good news for me?'

She shook her head. 'Not really! It's just that I was wondering if you'd thought any more about me going to France, that's all.?'

Mikael looked a little more serious now. 'Yes I have and want to know a bit more about just how you are going to do it. Are you really seriously fit enough to ride all that way on a bicycle at your age.?'

Rosanna nodded vigorously. 'Of course I am, every weekend now I go out with the club usually to the coast and back, this is well over a hundred miles.'

'And what about the Alps should you get that far, could you manage them?'

Rosanna smiled. 'Yes of course! I go out often with boys that have climbed them and beat them all the time.'

Mikael looked surprised at this he knew his daughter was a strong girl but this was a different situation. 'That sounds good but I still need to think about it a little longer, I'll probably let you know in a few weeks time when your passport comes back to me. Meanwhile you need to know a bit more about the wild food you might need on the way if you get stuck. There isn't much of it around these parts but I'll show you the poison ones as well.'

Rosanna looked pleased at this, things looked more promising now.

'Thank you father. I promise to make notes of all you show me and I'll start getting all my travelling clothes together.' She kissed him and said goodbye.

The following weeks were busy ones for Rosanna finding suitable clothes to travel with, she knew that the weather could be cold and wet especially in high altitudes. Sleeping on the way could be a problem but she was willing to work at farms on the journey to get by. Most of her equipment she bought very cheaply at Army Surplus stores, and although a bit heavy and rough should last the trip.

When the day finally arrived to depart as she knew it would come, the last words her father spoke after giving her twenty five pounds were. 'Promise me Rosanna to contact me at least once a month whatever happens so that I know you are are alive, safe, and well. If you are short of money don't hesitate to let me know and I will wire you some?'

Rosanna was almost in tears as she kissed him goodbye even feeling so happy to be off on a lifetimes adventure, not knowing just how good it was going to do her. Mikael waved her goodbye as she rode off knowing that she had at least been brought up to know right from wrong, and she would have the same chance of seeing the world as he had done all those years ago. It was now a hopefully a better world for her to grow up in, he wished more children could be able to do the same.

He knew that with luck and the way she coped with life in general Rosanna would get by no matter what happened, and that she'd come back a very positive person indeed.